Breach of the Peace

A Dag Meldel Tale

Copyright 2021

P F Damsberg

Also by the author:

Dag Meldel Detective Tales:
The Arcturus Code – Book 1
Hagal's Eight – Book 2
Kickback – Book 3
Lost Overboard – Book 4

The Lazuli Fantasy Series:
The Lazuli Stone – Part One
The Lazuli Brotherhood – Part Two
The Lazuli Crown – Part Three
The Lazuli Inheritance – Part Four
Lazuli ~ The Fall of Albia – Part Five

Young Adult Science Fiction:
The Riddle Of Red Rocks – Part One
The Quantum Agency – Part Two

Silas Daniel Dyer – Biographical History

Stories of Lost Souls – Short Story Omnibus

Sterngard's Words – Science Fantasy

1.

Dag stood, looking out of the wide window that framed the seascape that was the backdrop to his house. Not just the sea, but the sky as well. There was only a short stretch of grass he called a garden before the rocky ground came to an abrupt end at the lip of a cliff.

He had stood there for some time. Long enough for his hot black coffee to have become lukewarm. The triple glazed glass had not kept the sound of the wind from drowning out the ticking of the lounge clock. The grey and black clouds scudded low across the sea and leapt up, with the salty spray and spume, from the crashing waves to thrum against the glass along with the icy raindrops.

It was dark. Only the glow of a single table-side light spread across the walls of one corner of the room.

Dag suddenly shivered. His mind had been far away. He had watched the storm and felt its strength against the window, but his mind had become a blank. He came out of his reverie and out the mug of coffee to his lips only to grimace in distaste at the cold liquid. He liked it hot. He shivered again and realised his hands were cold as was the room. The heating turned off automatically at nine in the morning and come on again at six. He wasn't usually at home to need it on.

He shivered once more and went to the kitchen to turn it on and make a new hot mug of coffee, flicking the switches to turn on lights as he went.

He put the electric hob on, put water and freshly ground coffee into the percolator, and put it on to simmer. His cereal bowl was still in the sink, unwashed. He sighed, turned on the hot water and washed it. Small specks of the muesli had stuck to the bowl like concrete, and he had to scrub them off.

He didn't like the stuff. Fruit muesli they called it. He thought of it more as wood shavings and rabbit droppings. He had never usually eaten any breakfast; just a mug of hot black coffee was all he needed to start the day. But now he had to have something to eat, his stomach needed something inside it before he had the tablets. The consultant told him that he must do that, even though they had also given him pills to protect the stomach lining, as well as calcium tablets to protect his bones. All to counteract the harmful effects of the medication which was supposed to put things right.

He wasn't used to having so little to do. He had thought he'd made the right decision. He had had enough. His decision-making was slower than it had been, He wasn't seeing things as clearly as he used to. He was losing his edge, or so he thought. And he was getting tired more easily, more regularly.

He was about to quit, resign, tell them he'd had enough. He hadn't done it, not then, not impulsively, and it was a good thing he hadn't. If he had he would have forfeited his pension.

It had been pure chance. He'd been in an incident and afterwards was told to get a blood test, just to be sure. If he hadn't had that test he would never had known. If he hadn't had it he might no longer be alive, or at least things would be far worse than they were.

He was called in to the hospital just a day later. They took more blood, did more tests and then told him the news. It was not good news of course, somehow he didn't expect it to be, it was just a matter of what it was and how severe.

He had to see two consultants. They had not discovered just one problem but two. Firstly, it was his kidneys; acute kidney injury with tubulointerstitial nephritis. In other words they were not working properly, in fact, barely ten percent. They gave him the tablets for that. But, secondly, they found that he had lymphoma or lymphocytic leukaemia. In other words cancer, cancer of the white blood cells. Luckily – he always smiled at that word – it was not severe although he was reprimanded for not having gone to see his own doctor when he had originally noticed the lumps on his neck, and the steroids he was taking for the kidneys were reducing the lymph nodes and halting the progress of the cancer.

At least it had given him the opportunity to leave the force. He didn't have to tender his resignation just because he'd had enough and thought he was losing his edge, that he was slowing down and tired – which was because of the kidney problem anyway. He could leave as a result of his medical conditions, and that would also mean a pension.

The one thing that pleased him was that Martin Sorensen, his old Sergeant now an Inspector, had returned to Kristiansund to take his place.

And so, here he was at home, getting up later than he ever usually did, drinking coffee, and staring out of the window at a passing storm.

He made his coffee, turned on the central heating that he would never normally have on in the day time, then sat down in the lounge, switching on the television more for the background as noise as anything else. He needed to do something, but what? What could he do here in Kristiansund? He hadn't ever had any hobbies as such, so nothing he could immediately turn to now he had so much spare time. He had gone out and ended up in the bar frequented by the old crew, but he was no longer part of it, and they all treated him as if he handicapped in some way, always asking if he needed to sit or suggesting that he ought not to have another drink. He felt fine. In fact, he hadn't felt so well for a long time, but maybe that was because he was now fully rested. Why did people treat him as if he was infirm? Were they sorry for him? Did they pity him?

It was Kristiansund. It was small, or rather, it was not large. You couldn't hide in a place like this. Everyone knew you and knew your business, especially if you'd had a high profile and were well known. But what to do?

For now, he was at a loss.

The TV had flickered into life. It was eleven o'clock. Dag had it on the 24 hour news channel and they were just moving over from sports new to the main news headlines. Dag guessed what the main headline would be. The previous day there had been intense speculation as to who or what organisation would be awarded the Nobel Peace prize, and today was the day that it would be announced.

Peace; Dag snorted at the word. When had there ever been peace? And some of the people they had given it to in the past had been pretty controversial. A couple still in power in their countries had sullied the prize's reputation. However, he had to admit that an organisation like the World Food Programme was a good choice, and individuals such as Nelson Mandela, undoubtedly good.

The presenter announced they were cutting to the announcement being made by the Chair of the Norwegian Noble Committee.

Dag put his mug down on the coffee table and picked up the local newspaper hoping it would be more interesting, but was dubious.

The voice of the Chair intoned her prepared speech in the background.

The headline in the paper was about a new road and tunnel that had been completed several months ago but had still not opened for some inexplicable reason. Turning over, on the sports page, was a Manchester United player defending their manager, Kristiansund's own Ole Gunnar Solskjær, against attacks on his poor performance.

In the background the Chair paused in her speech to give extra impact to the revealing of the winner's name.

Dag looked up from the paper.

" .. peace prize to ...... Jamba Caleb Rakha,"

Dag frowned. Who on earth was he?

The Chair continued, explaining the reasons why he had been chosen.

Dag remembered now. A leader of a small country which had been immersed in civil war since, it seemed, 1945. A never-ending conflict between different tribes and religions in a part of the world the rest of it had all but forgotten. Until Jamba Caleb Rakha came along. He had brought together the disparate groups and, against the odds, managed to conduct a reasonably fair election to a newly set-up parliament, pronounced such by independent observers mostly from Europe and America, but also South Africa who had more self-centred reasons to see peace there.

Dag mentally shrugged. Wait and see how long that peace lasts, he thought.

2.

Time had gone by in a blur. The days had passed without there being any real separation between them; one day being much like any other. Then, days had become weeks. A month had gone by.

It was a clear bright morning, cold and frosty, but far better than being cold and damp, when Dag received the phone call. It was Anders his brother-in-law, husband to his only sibling, his sister Kristine.

It was bad news. It had all happened very suddenly. One day, she was as well as always, and the next she was lying in a hospital bed. In the few days that she had remaining Anders had been too upset and preoccupied to call Dag, so he said. Although Dag had never kept in close contact with her or Anders except at, perhaps, Christmas and Easter, and he had never got around visiting them in Slependen, West of Oslo, where they now lived. She had asked him to visit on the card she had sent him the previous Christmas. Anders said it was a brain tumour of some sort.

Many times before it had been Dag's job to tell people of the loss of a loved one. Not since his parents had died had it been his turn to be on the receiving end.

He, like those he had told before, was lost for words for a few seconds.

"I'm sorry, Anders." He said. "I can't believe it, she was always so fit and careful about her health, wasn't she?"

"Yes. Yes. She was." Anders replied, but Dag could tell he was finding it difficult to speak.

"I must come to Slependen. Do you know yet when the funeral may be?"

"Not for another week."

"Well, I'll make plans. I won't trouble you, I'll book into a hotel."

"You may stay here if you wish."

"No, it's OK, I'm not in the best of states myself at the moment. I'll find a hotel."

"What is it, what's the matter?"

Dag had not told his sister what had happened to him. He had not wanted to worry her. He couldn't face telling her he fact that his life may only have limited time left. And now, her own had ended.

"Oh, nothing much, I had to take early retirement. I'd had enough."

"I see. Well, I'll email you the details. Kristine had your address."

"I'll see you then." Dag told him.

Dag had never got on well with Anders. In fact, he had been surprised that Kristine had put up with him for so many years. It was the unspoken reason that he preferred not to stay at Anders' house, although his nephew and niece and their young children would be there anyway so there'd be little room. He thought about them as well as he made himself another coffee. He hadn't kept in contact with his nephew and niece much over the years either, and now he was beginning to regret it.

Maybe, he could put things right, or at least keep in better contact with them in future – or what was left of it.

It was the next day that Anders sent an email giving him the details of the funeral. It was on the following Thursday, in six days time. He went straight onto his laptop and looked for flights to Oslo. There was a flight each morning at 08:55, and he picked the one for the Wednesday morning before the funeral. Unusually he chose a single fare, he just didn't know then when he might want to return home. It was more expensive, getting on for twice as much, but Dag was unconcerned. Then, he had to decide where to stay. There was a hotel not too far away from where they lived in Slependen situated on the Olsofjord. But, when he checked where the crematorium was he found it was about 8k's away in the hills back towards central Oslo; a fair taxi journey or a roundabout bus ride. It was about twice the distance from central Oslo to the crematorium, but at least he'd not be stuck in an out-of-the-way hotel with little else to do. It was one simple journey by train from the airport to Oslo, and it only took twenty-five minutes. So, next he chose a hotel, one near the Central Station; he didn't like trekking from there to the hotel once he'd arrived.

He was surprised that the old Comfort Hotel Grand Central at the station itself was so cheap. It had all the amenities, it looked comfortable, and was perfectly adequate for him. He booked it for a week. Maybe, he would leave early, maybe he would hang around for a while, perhaps to see the family again.

Strangely, although it was not a good reason for feeling better, for his spirits being raised, he was, and they were. It had given him a reason for setting his mind to doing something, for pulling him out of his melancholic day to day existence. At last he had something to do, a purpose.

That night he even went into town and to the pub where the police tended to congregate.

A few of them were there. He nodded amiably to them, replied to their questions to say he was feeling fine, bought a drink, and sat by himself at a table unfolding and reading his paper for at least the third time that day. He hated just sitting and drinking, he needed a newspaper to avoid staring about the room.

There was the sound of footsteps and he looked up. It was Martin Sorensen, his old Sergeant, now the Inspector sitting at his old desk.

"Dag! How are you? You've not been seen for weeks, I was

14

wondering is you were OK. I should have called in on you, but well, I've been getting my feet under the table."

Dag smiled. "I'm fine thanks, been taking it easy for the first time in I don't know how long. How is my old desk by the way?"

Martin grinned. "My legs are longer than yours I think. I have to get a bigger one."

"Bigger desks for bigger responsibilities, eh?"

"It's not easy to fill your shoes, Dag. Anyway, have what have you been up to besides taking it easy, you must have found something to do?"

"No not really. I'm having to go to Oslo next week, though."

"Oh why's that?"

"My sister. She's passed away. Quite suddenly."

"Oh I'm sorry to hear that. Was she younger or older ....." He began but didn't finish. "Sorry, that was probably not the right way to put it, considering."

"No need to worry about stepping on eggshells with me, and anyway everything's under control. I've years left in me yet. But, as you asked, she was older, five years older."

"Oslo." Martin said, and frowned. "There was a call from Oslo for you the other day. One of the constables took it. Didn't leave a name or contact number though, just asked for you by name."

Dag shrugged,. "Maybe something about my Sister. Her husband called me in the end. We never got on. But I'll have to do my best at the funeral, or rather cremation."

Someone was calling for Martin and he turned around to see who it was. "I'd better go. But we must keep in contact, more than we have done so far. Let me know when you're back from Oslo, we'll meet up."

Dag agreed. He finished a second drink and then headed back home nodding to a few of them as he left.

3.

It was pitch dark, and early in the morning when Dag took the taxi to the airport. There had been a light snowfall during the night but it was now turning to rain. The sun will have risen before the plane took off, and he would be flying in daylight, and he would be at Oslo airport before 10:00 needn't rush after that as he couldn't book into the hotel officially until midday at the earliest and, if the room wasn't ready, not until 14:00.

As it happened the flight was delayed for almost an hour. They landed at 11:45 and it was 12:15 before Dag dragged his bag from the carousel. Domestic arrivals exited directly onto a small concourse and the escalator to the train station. But it was lunchtime, and he'd not eaten since the mush early in the morning, so he stopped opposite them, bought a baguette and sat and ate it with a doubtful cup of coffee.

Only partly satisfied he headed doe to catch the train. He should be in Oslo Central Station by 13:30 and judged that he had a good chance of booking into his room without too much of a wait.

The train pulled into Central Station. Dag alighted and, without having to look for the exit was able to following the well-seasoned travellers who knew their way. He waited at the bottom of an escalator not rushing to push through the small bunch of people who'd gathered, and waited for it to ease, then got on it putting his suitcase on the step in front. At the top he picked it up and stepped off the moving stair, walked a step or two, put it down to pull out the handle. As he did so, he momentarily blocked the way to the down escalator. As he pulled the handle he was roughly bumped into. There was a gruff, murmured apology, and by the time Dag looked up the person was already heading down the escalator and disappearing behind several other bodies. But from the corner of his eye he had seen something fall from the person or the bag slung over their shoulder.

Dag grunted. Then, he looked down at what had fallen at his feet. He picked it up. It was a tourist map. He looked back to the escalator. The person was now long gone. He grunted again, then began to pull his suitcase along to find out where the hotel entrance was. It couldn't be far away. It was, after all, almost part of the station. He looked for a bin to put the map in but didn't immediately see one, so he slid it into his coat pocket. He could get rid of it later.

It wasn't long before he was in the hotel lobby and checking in. Luckily his room was already available, so he wouldn't have to wait around in reception.

He took his black suit out of the bag and put it in the wardrobe along with his black tie and white shirt, and a spare pair of jeans. His other clothes he put in a chest of drawers. He had hung his coat on the peg on the bedroom door, and noticed the map poking out of the pocket. He took it out. He almost threw it into the bin but changed his mind. It would come in useful. He had everything he needed on his phone these days, but there was something about a real paper map that a phone's screen never really encapsulated. He placed it on the dressing table come writing desk for later. It was now gone 14:30 and there would only be another hour and a half of daylight remaining. He would take a look around the local area but leave any more serious sightseeing until the day after tomorrow – after the funeral.

The map remained on the table.

After breakfast the next morning Dag asked at the reception the best way to get to the crematorium. He was surprised that there was a here was a bus service, the number 150, which would take him from just up the road at the National Theatre all the way to Haslum and just a short walk to the crematorium. It would cost just over 100 krone. When he asked about a taxi, he was told it would be more like 320 krone. The taxi would take about 20 minutes, the bus about 45 minutes and ran every quarter of an hour. He looked at his watch. He had plenty of time. The service wasn't until 11:30. He decided to save money and take his time; the bus would do.

He caught the bus at at 10:24. It would arrive at 11:06 and would give him plenty of time for the short walk to the crematorium and be early enough to be respectful and meet whoever was there, but not too early and leaving him hanging about outside.

He had misread Anders' email. Kristine would be cremated at the crematorium, and it would be where her ashes would be laid to rest, but the preceding service was at the nearby church. A few minutes extra walk away. By the time he arrived there was already a small crowd congregating outside the door.

He looked around at the faces. There was no-one he particularly recognised. Unknown faces, friends, relatives perhaps, that he had no knowledge of, whom he had never met or had any contact with. Kristine was his sister, but he was the odd one out.

It was Anders who came over and spoke to him first, his son and daughter in tow.

Anders was polite. His face was strained. He was so much older than Dag remembered. But, there again, so was he. His nephew and niece, who had been young faces in photographs were now grown, strangers to him. But Finn, the young man, shook his hand firmly and said how pleased he was to meet him. He had read about his cases in the papers and asked what he was now working on. Dag had to admit that he had now retired and his days of interesting cases had finished. Finn said he was sorry to hear it; he had wanted to join the police but his mother had been against it. Dag was not surprised, she would have thought that Finn may have become like him. By then both Anders and his daughter Anette had wandered back to the other mourners. Finn had seemed reluctant to join them and lingered with Dag.

"Where are you staying?" Finn asked.

"At a hotel in town."

"Will you be leaving right after the service?"

"I expect so. I don't know anyone here, other than

yourselves of course. I think I'd be a bit out of place."

Finn gave a nod. "My father's never been easy to get on with. It's a shame you hadn't kept in touch. I'd have liked that."

Dag gave a nod and a faint smile. "As things stand, I think I would have like that as well. I'm pretty much alone these days."

"How long are you staying in town?"

"I haven't actually made any plans; a few days at least. Thought I'd do some sightseeing, museums and such."

"Perhaps we could meet up and I could show you around?"

Dag looked at Finn. He seemed to be, not just asking, but appealing to him in a way. Dag had seen it many times before in the force. Someone wanting to talk but not saying so openly.

Dag nodded and smiled. "Yes, that would be good. I'm staying at the Comfort Hotel Grand Central, it's at Central Station. Here," he added, "this is my phone number." and handed him a card.

"I'll give you a call." Finn managed to say before his father called him over and he had to go.

The mourners were then called into the church.

It wasn't a long service. People stood and talked of Kristine's life; a life he had known very little about. It was much like a story-telling to Dag. It wasn't, to him, a telling of a life he knew or recognised. He was not part of it.

People congregated outside afterwards, talking in small

groups, then moving on to to form new one's. Dag stood to the side of it all. After some minutes he'd had enough and sought out Anders to say goodbye. They shook hands, politely said their farewells, and Dag extracted himself from the small group that Anders was with. Anette had almost pointedly ignored him.

But as he walked away Finn came up to him again.

"I'll give you a call later, Uncle Dag."

Dag turned and smiled. "Yes, sure, I'd like that." Then turned and walked past the crematorium and back to the bus stop. There was, for the first time, tears welling in his eyes. He took a deep breath, blew his nose, and carried on walking.

He needed a drink when he got back to the hotel. Still attired in his black suit, white shirt and black tie he sat in the bar and had a large whisky, then another. He looked at his watch. It late afternoon and he hadn't eaten, and now he was drinking on an empty stomach. He knew that wouldn't do. He must find somewhere to get a snack at least. First he went back to his room and changed.

He was ready to go out again. The room had been serviced but, Dag noticed, the tourist map still rested on the table. He would use that tomorrow, but picked it up to take with him. Her needed something to look a t whilst he had some food. There was nothing worse than sitting down eating somewhere on your own staring blankly around you, and Dag thought it even worse to be engrossed in a mobile phone screen.

However, he did a quick check on his phone first for places

to eat. There were a plethora of cafes and restaurants in the area, but so many of them were Thai, Indian or Burger joints, and he didn't fancy them. He wanted a traditional meal of some sort. Luckily he spotted a traditional if not 'old-fashioned' dining room only ten minutes walk away which opened at 16:30.

He was shown to a table. The waitress took his coat, and he quickly remembered to take the map out of the pocket and put it on the table beside him, and ordered a beer. He looked at the menu and made some quick choices; lemon and king crab with lemon cream and salad to start followed by Filét of veal with asparagus, cabbage with morels, onion sauce and fried potatoes. He was treating himself.

His beer came, and he picked up the tourist map for something to look at whilst he drank it and waited for the starter.

He opened it out awkwardly. It was difficult to open it out fully without taking over more than the entire table. He folded it so that he could see just the central parts of the city where most of the tourist sights were. He found his hotel and scanned the area around. Oslo Cathedral was close to his hotel and was a good central starting point. Heading towards the Royal palace there was the Parliament, neither interested him particularly, but he could walk by. The National Gallery and Historical Museum were just to the North of them, he might go there. South towards the docks and fjord were two new museums and the new National Museum which was still under construction. Just to one side of them was the Rådhuset; the city's town hall. A great red-bricked building opened in 1950 to one side of which were two large twin towers.

It was then that Dag noticed the marks on the map. Only small pen marks, but each precisely pricked upon the surface at points on and around the Rådhuset. He looked at them more closely, but his inspection was interrupted by the arrival of his starter. He was one of only three tables occupied and it hadn't taken the kitchen long to prepare it. He folded the map and put it out of the way, but the marks intrigued him. He was impatient take another look.

The stater was excellent. He had finished his beer and put up his hand to order a glass of red wine to go with the veal, then reopened the map.

He held it up to a light. Yes, the marks were there and they looked precise. And Dag knew almost immediately the reason for them being there. Whoever had made the marks had no done so for touristic reasons. The positions of the marks could only be indication where there may be security cameras. He looked at the rest of the map. There were no other marks as far as he could tell. Then, he suddenly thought of finger prints. Here he was leaving his all over it and maybe disturbing those already on the map without taking any precautions at all. He carefully refolded the map using his handkerchief just as his main course and wine arrived.

The main course would have been as excellent as the first if only his mind and taste buds were concentrating on it, but, of course, his mind was not. The picture of the pen marks, probably marking where there were security cameras had taken over his thoughts. He would have to go and check out the area as soon as his meal was over.

At the end of the meal the waitress asked if he wanted coffee. For once he declined. He was keen to to take a look around the City Hall, and it was only another ten minutes walk further away from the hotel.

There was a semi-circular 'square' in from of the two towers. Dag took out his map. In front of the two towers the offices formed another semi enclosed square with a fountain in the middle of it which opened out onto the main square. The two marks that were slightly heavier than the others were on each of the two protruding office blocks. Dag walked over to take a closer look. It was as he suspected. A covered walkway lined each of the blocks. The annotations were each where a security camera was placed in the corner of the blocks, each surveying the courtyard.

He checked out the others marks. Each was the same. Each noted a position of a security camera. It total, Dag estimated, the cameras would have covered most of the courtyard and the the 'square'. Although, maybe not all of it. As he walked around trying to act like a tourist he tried to establish if there was any dead ground, any area where someone could not been seen. And if there was, or if there were more than one, could there be a track that a person could take where they would always be out of shot?

It was dark now, and trying to work that our wouldn't be possible. In fact he would have to have access to the camera details to be able to work it out and be sure of it. However, somcone with a good knowledge of such things, and perhaps having got the details of the cameras and lenses in use, or have a useful contact of the inside of the observers, could work it out.

He realised, suddenly, that he was thinking like his old self again. He had, in his hands, a piece of evidence, a map that had accidentally come into his possession, and his mind had worked out what it meant. It meant that this was most definitely a police matter.

There was a pub at the corner of one of the semi-circular buildings around the 'square'. Dag needed another drink and time to think. In reality he should not have taken time to think, he should simply have passed the matter tot the police. But, he already had the feeling that if this was presented to him, he would not think it the most compelling evidence.; and he had no idea who had dropped it, nor could he even describe who they were.

Drinking and thinking was definitely required, not that the two should always go hand in hand.

After the second drink, Dag looked at his watch and decided that there would be no point in going to a police station to report what he believed, and the likelihood was that they would not take it too seriously either. After all, if he had been presented with it by a member of the public on a cold November night, he would simply have put in in his in tray for the next day, and even then it would probably be covered by more serious incident reports.

What he needed was a contact. Then he remembered a D.I. He was in contact with over the missing boy case, the one who was supposed to have been lost overboard. What was his name? He searched his address book on the phone. He'd not deleted any of the contacts even though he should have scrapped the work one's. There he was; D.I. Solberg, and his phone number.

He tried it. It went onto messages. Dag left him a message asking that he meet with him preferably the next day, and left it at that.

He ordered another drink and promised himself it would be his last and then he'd go back to his hotel.

4.

Dag was awoken by the buzzing of his phone which was, for some reason, secreted under his pillow. He grabbed it and it nearly flew out of his hand; it was connected to the recharging cable which was too short for him to put the phone to his ear. He turned over on his side and put his head on the side of the bed to put the phone to his ear.

"Hello?" He asked, his voice sounding rough and dry.

"Dag Meldel?"

"Speaking." He answered and pulled himself on to the edge of the bed to sit.

"It's D.I. Bjørn Solberg, you left a message for me."

Dag looked at his watch. It was only just seven. "You're early."

"We've got a job on; early start."

"I see, well, I think I may have come across something which may be important, but unfortunately it may not be seen so by a desk Sergeant. I needed someone to talk to with a bit more authority."

"Is see. And someone who knows your reputation and wouldn't dismiss what ever it is out of hand?"

"That's about the sum of it, yes."

"How long are you around for?"

"I'm booked into my hotel for another five days."

"Oh, that's no problem then. I'll see how this job goes today and, with a bit of luck, can meet up with you this evening. At the very latest tomorrow."

Dag thanked him. The first thing he needed to do now was get a drink of water. He tried to remember what he'd drunk last night. He could recall the first three drinks but after that it became a bit hazy. It was not like him. He promised himself, looking at the grey and haggard face in the mirror, that it should not happen again. He must stick to coffee.

The thought of coffee and the time spurred him on to get ready and have an early breakfast. Not muesli this time, something more substantial. He needed some food inside his stomach, then back to his room to take his pills. After that he would give Finn a call and find out what sightseeing he had in mind.

Finn arrived at the hotel 10:00, bright-eyed, and raring to go. Dag had been sat waiting in an armchair in reception. He was looking at the map again, but being very careful, holding it whilst wearing a pair of black leather gloves for the outdoors. The weather crisp, clear, and cold.

"Morning Uncle Dag! Not much need for that map, I know my way around."

Finn had surprised him as he studied the map.

"Ah, there you are. The map? No, it's not mine. Well, it is now, but it wasn't. I just need to hang onto it until this evening." Dag told Finn, whilst folding the map and putting it inside a plastic folder he'd managed to scrounge from reception.

"You're taking good care of it. Why this evening?"

"I have to give it to a friend."

Finn looked at him and his brow wrinkled. "Sounds a bit suspicious. What's so special about it, it's just an old tourist map? And who's the friend? Anyone interesting?"

Dag sighed, then smiled. "You ask more questions than a detective, and as inquiring. I might tell you about it later, but, come one, we're supposed to be sightseeing."

Oslo is not a big city, not like London where Dag had gone for his last and one of his rare holidays which had not ended up like a holiday at all; he'd fallen into a case pressed upon him by his superiors and the agent from E14, the Norwegian Intelligence Service. Central Oslo and all it had to offer was within a 5K by 2K area, not spread out into so many districts as a city as big as London. Within it were all the sights, museums and galleries he'd want to see. The only place he wanted to visit that was a little further away was the Viking Ship Museum and the Polar Ship Museum on the peninsular of land that jutted out into the fjord, Bygdøy. Dag said that he'd leave that until the next day.

It was early afternoon, and they had not stopped for lunch. Both were feeling hungry. Dag agreed to stop for something to eat. He had manoeuvred the tour so that they were getting close to the City Hall and took Finn to the pub he'd been before for a drink and food; coffee this time he promised himself, and not alcohol. From there it gave him the chance to look out onto the semi-circular pedestrianised piazza.

Both of them settled for a dish of prawns and rice, and Dag relented to please Finn and ordered them both a beer, just a half for himself but a large one for Finn.

As they drank and ate Dag kept looking out of the window. Finn asked him why. Dag pulled the map from his pocket, put on his gloves, and pulled it out of the plastic jacket.

Finn frowned. "Why are you doing that?" Then, his eyes lit up. "Is it to do with a case? Are you making sure you're not damaging any fingerprints?" He said eagerly.

Dag looked him in the eye. "Yes, that's exactly it."

For Dag it was suddenly like having his Detective Sergeant to speak to. He needed that, he wasn't able to keep this to himself. He had been unsure of his competence and he wanted reassurance, support for what he thought had discovered, even though he couldn't be sure what that was; and Finn was there.

He told Finn how it had come into his possession. Then told him that he'd marks he'd found on it. Finn wanted to see, so Dag told him to put his gloves on and then opened up the map. Hc had not told Finn exactly what he had found and asked Finn what he could see.

Finn studied it. His brow furrowed, and his eyes narrowed. Then, the lines cleared and his eyes lit up.

"There!" He said. "There's some marks there."

Finn looked at the map again and then out of the window. "It's here." He said. "That's why you came here for lunch. What are they?"

"When we go back outside you can see for yourself. I don't think you'll find it difficult." Dag smiled, and folded the map away.

Finn watched him out the map in his pocket and looked out into the piazza. Dag's eyes followed Finn's. A young woman was running past, attractive enough to take any young man's attention. As she ran past she looked around for a brief moment and carried on running quickly going out of sight.

For a second Dag's heart jumped. It was the face. He knew the face. The young woman was someone he knew, or at least had come across before. But who was she?

"What's the matter, Uncle Dag, you've gone quite pale." Finn asked.

"The young lady who ran past just then. I recognised her."

"Really? From Kristiansund perhaps?"

Dag;s eyes almost closed as he thought. He tried to picture that face again. He knew he had seen her before, and he also that it must be important.

Dag's eyes opened wide. "Ingrid!" He said loudly. "Ingrid, the Receptionist at Flåm Hotel. Well, not just a receptionist, as we found out. What the hell is she doing here, in Oslo?"

"Is she from one of your cases?" Finn asked.

"Yes, but not one you will have heard much about. A dead body that turned up in a village , then disappeared. After that, all sorts of things happened."

"The dead body and those missing guys. Wasn't that when a woman was shot dead? Something happening on board that cruise ship?"

Dag raised both eyebrows. "You really have kept a check on my cases. That was one which they kept as quiet as possible."

"Why's that?"

"Because foreign agents were involved. And that young woman we just saw was one of them. I'm going to have to get word to someone I know."

"Let's go after her." Finn said, standing.

"She'll be long gone by now. But I'll make that call."

For the second time in a couple of days he was looking for a phone number on his address book that he had not used for some time. It was just a Christian name; Rolf.

The number rang, but there was no reply, nor did it go to a voice message. That didn't surprise Dag. He was sure it would be picked up, and he'd get an answer later.

Dag paid the bill and they went outside.

"You go and see what those marks were. I'll follow." Dag told Finn.

Finn walked around the piazza and came to the first of the cameras, looked up and saw it. He nodded and smiled, then went over to the next, smiled again and carried on.

"So, each of the security cameras have been marked on that map." He concluded. Looking pleased with himself.

Dag nodded. "Correct."

"What are you doing about it. I mean why has someone done that? A robbery, a murder, or," then his eyes did go wide, "a terrorist attack!"

"I'm beginning to think the latter, but there's nothing really to go on, no evidence, other than those marks, and any possible prints on it."

"And the person who bumped into you and dropped it." Finn added.

"Yes, and for that I need to get the Oslo police involved. If they take it seriously they can go through the security cameras and try and find out if they can identify the person. I know the time almost exactly so it should be easy enough."

"Ah, and that's who you're meeting tonight. Someone in the Oslo Police." Finn asked him.

"Yes, I thought it was better to use a contact rather than being an ordinary member of the public reporting a pretty fanciful story."

Dag looked at his watch. "let's call it a day. I want to be available if my contact gets in touch with me."

"Can't I come along?" Finn asked. "I've nothing better to do than take the bus back home, and I'd sooner not go."

"You don't want to go home? Why?"

Finn gave a look of misery. "Father makes it worse than ever now that mum's gone. I can't stand it."

Dag stopped and looked at Finn. "Maybe he's hurting. Maybe he's feeling her loss more than you think. It's not going to be easy for him, you know."

Finn gave him an odd look. "He doesn't really care. He's just angry, angry that he's got us around and mum's not there to take care of things."

Dag frowned, it sounded worse than he thought. He always thought there was something not quite right with his sister's relationship, but never knew what it was. He could ask Finn now, get down to the bottom of it, but it wasn't quite the right time or place. He would leave it for later, but he would relent and let Finn stay with him a little longer, let him go home when he felt more comfortable about it.

"OK, let's go back to my hotel and get into the warm and have a coffee. I can wait there to hear from him."

They had only just finished their coffee, sat in the comfortable reception armchairs, when Dag's phone rang. It was D.I. Solberg. He told Dag that he would see him in just twenty minutes. That was how long it would take him to walk from the Oslo police Headquarters to the train station. He chose one of the bars in the station for them to meet rather than the hotel. Dag knew why. No-one took much notice of the people coming, going, and hanging around a train station bar. It was an anonymous flow of ever-changing faces, people going about their lives without much of a thought to anyone else around them.

"You have to let me come." Finn insisted. "I know all about it now anyway. There's no point keeping out of it."

A point well-made, thought Dag, so he agreed.

They met at the Sidesporet Pub on an upper level not far from platform 10 where the airport train had deposited Dag.

Dag looked around as he entered and saw Bjorn stand up then sit as he knew Dag had seen him. Dag and Finn went over and took seats at his table.

Bjorn gave Finn and enquiring look and Dag told him that it was Finn and that he knew all about the matter.

35

Bjorn shrugged and asked him what it was all about, which Dag explained and passed the map in its plastic folder to him. Bjorn opened it, carefully using a paper napkin and took a look.

"Not much to go on. In fact, nothing at all, just a suspicion that there might be something criminal or otherwise to it. But, to be honest, nothing that's going to warrant and full scale inquiry."

"I realise that." Admitted Dag. "But perhaps a check on any prints at least?"

Bjorn gave a nod. "As it's you, and I know you wouldn't be passing this to me unless you thought it necessary, I'll get that done. After all, you do have a nose for things, don't you. I'll get back to you as soon as I can. But, as you know, it can take a couple of days. They're short-staffed as always."

"I'll be around for a few days yet." Dag told him.

Bjorn didn't stay for a drink even. He was on his way again right away with the map.

"That's not going to get us very far is it Uncle?"

"He'll do what he can. But it's a long shot no matter what."

"Odd thing, though," Finn considered aloud, "you could probably see everything you needed to on Google Earth or Street View, you'd hardly have to mark it out on a map."

Dag pursed his lips. He hadn't thought of that. "Do you think so?"

"Have you got a computer?"

"My laptop's in my room."

"Well, come on, let's have a look!" Finn enthused.

Dag sighed. The keenness of youth. He was unused to it. "OK, let's have a look, but it won't tell us anything we don't know will it?"

"It may do, you never know."

Dag was mildly surprised. The satellite image of Oslo was surprisingly good and clear, Finn changed the perspective to 3D and zoomed in,which brought the buildings incredibly close and detailed. Some of the cameras could be made out, although not clearly enough for Dag to have definitely made them out without prior knowledge. The street view was even better. The cameras were distinctly visible, especially the one's hidden under the roof of the walkway around the City hall courtyard. They would not have been seen from the air. So, the question was why did someone need to mark them out on the map?

"Maybe they're as good as I am at using computers?" Dag suggested satirically.

"Or they just wanted to make sure, take a last look." said Finn.

"Yes, a final recce before doing whatever it is they have planned. Which is disturbing. It means that whatever it is could be quite close. Is there anything going on at the City Hall in the near future? Take a look online."

Finn searched. He used one search engine and then another. "Nothing very soon. In fact, nothing for quite a while."

"Maybe there are some important guests, visitors, which wouldn't necessarily be on the internet." Dag surmised. "We'd need someone on the inside to find out."

"Kenneth might know." Suggested Finn.

"Kenneth?"

"We were at school together. He works for the City Council now; in the planning department."

A thought struck Dag. "Talking of work, what do you do? Or what are you supposed to be doing? I'd imagined you'd been given time off because of your mother."

Finn a little abashed. "I gave up my job just before it happened. I'm looking for something new."

"What was it you did?" Dag asked him.

Finn shrugged. "I was a trainee manager at a supermarket. I couldn't stand another day of it. I thought – well - I thought I might apply for the police now. Father won't stand in my way. I won't let him. I only kept myself from doing it because mum didn't want me to."

"Ah, I see. So, you have plenty of time on your hands them?"

"It means I can help you." Finn looked at his Uncle with a glint in his eye.

"Hmm, I suppose it does. Can you get to see this Kenneth tomorrow do you think?"

"Yes, I'm sure. If I could buy him lunch, that is." Finn looked hopeful.

Dag gave a shake of his head but pulled out his wallet. "There," he said, passing him some notes, "I still find myself having to pay for information. Now," He looked at his watch. "The tome's getting on. You must get back home. We'll meet up tomorrow morning, and if there's no word from your Kenneth, we'll go take a look at the Viking Ship and Polar Museums. By the time we've done that I might have had word back from Bjørn."

5.

Finn phoned Dag just after he had breakfasted. He had called Kenneth the night before. Kenneth was wary about giving out information but Finn had spun him a good yarn that his Uncle was a famous Detective, and he was helping him with an important case together with the Oslo Police, but it was a very confidential matter and had to be kept out of the press, which was why his Uncle was involved. Still dubious, but giving way, Kenneth agreed to find out if any important visitors were due in the next week or two.

All they could do was wait and see if Kenneth came up with something, so carried on with Dag's plan to see the museums.

They heard nothing that morning from either Kenneth or Bjørn. They had lunch near the Fram Museum, that with the polar exploration ship as well as a Northern Lights show. They both had sausages with potato bread and coffee which Dag was surprised to find was exceptionally go, so ended up having three full cups.

After they had finished, both left text messages for their contacts.

"Not much else to do but wait." Dag told Finn. "Shall we take another look around the City Hall area, you never know we may have missed something?"

A number 30 bus took them all the way there and thirty-five minutes later they were standing once again in the piazza looking as best they could like tourists. Another twenty minute walk around ,and they had discovered nothing else.

"The pub on the corner?" Finn suggested.

The day was getting colder and Dag admitted he could do with being in the warm.

They had hoped to get a table by the window but they were all taken and had to settle for one at the rear of the room. There was extra room on a balcony but Dag grunted his disapproval when Finn suggested climbing the stairs.

When they sat at the table with their drinks that they'd bought and collected at the bar, Dag's phone rang. It was Bjørn.

Dag listened and, as he did so, his brow furrowed. All he said sever times was 'I see'.

Finn wondered what what Bjørn was telling Dag.

The call ended. Dag sat back with the phone still in his hand and his brow still creased, a thoughtful and puzzled look on his face.

"What is it? What's happened?" Finn asked him.

"It may be nothing, probably just an admin error, which happens sometimes." Dag said.

Finn waited, now puzzled himself. "And?"

Dag leaned forward. "The map." He said. "It was sent for finger printing. They got the results, or rather, they got prints from it, but none that matched anything on the computer system."

"So that's a bit of a dead-end than?"

"Hmm. Seems like it. But Bjørn asked for the map back, and when he did, they couldn't find it. It had gone missing. As I said, maybe just an admin error."

Finn looked at him and, as they often did, his eyes widened and lit up. "But, you don't believe that, do you? Someone's got their hands on it haven't they?"

"It's possible. But don't get carried away. These things do happen."

"How often?" Finn pressed him.

"Well," replied Dag, "sometimes. But also, sometimes, I have a nose for this sort of thing. And I'm not liking it."

"A mole! Inside the police department! It has to be!" Finn said enthusiastically.

"Shhh." Said Dag putting a finger to his lips, "Not so loud."

"Sorry." Finn apologised. And then his eyes veered to look above Dag's shoulder.

A shadow fell across Dag from the light on the wall near to them. Someone was standing behind him. He turned and looked.

"Yes, young man, you really shouldn't speak so loudly, anyone could hear you. Well, I could for one." Said the owner of the shadow.

"Rolf." Dag said with an deep exhale of breath.

Rolf pointed to the spare chair. "Do you mind?"

"Please do." Said Dag. "I thought you may have phoned me."

"I fancied a walk out, away from the office. It's not far from here you know." Rolf sat and looked at Dag. "I'm sorry to hear about your sister." Then he turned into Finn's eyes. "This must be your nephew, Finn?"

Finn nodded and Dag said, "Yes."

Rolf was Dag's Intelligence Agent (E14) contact whom he'd worked with on a case a few years earlier, had been involved in with the London case, and whom he had tried to call on his mobile.

"You called, wanted to talk to me about something." Rolf said, looking askance at Finn.

"I've told Finn, he was there, there's nothing to hide." Dag told him.

"Hmm, very well, carry on."

Dag did not ask him how he knew to find them at the pub, but he could guess. As soon as Dag had phone him Rolf would have made inquiries about where he was, found the hotel, and even had him followed. It wouldn't have taken Rolf long, Dag explained that they had been sitting in the very same pub, near the window, when he spotted a young woman hurrying, almost running, past. It had taken him a while to remember where he had seen her before, too late to catch up or follow her, but he was as sure as he could be that she was Ingrid, the receptionist at the hotel in Flåm a few years before, and redoubtably an agent of some foreign power or, at the least, someone working for whoever paid the best.

Rolf listened, but looked somewhat puzzled. Or, at least, as puzzled as he might ever look, which was very hardly showing any emotion at all.

Dag had noticed. "You look a bit perplexed."

"I am. What you have told me is very interesting, but it's not what I thought you had called me about."

It was Dag's turn to look puzzled. "Why, what did you think I may have called you about?"

"Why, the map, of course."

"The map?" Dag frowned. "How do you know about the map?"

"How do you think?"

"Ah." Said Dag, the answer dawning on him. "My map which has gone missing?"

"I wouldn't say missing." Rolf told him, looking hurt. "Requisitioned for further analysis would be the more appropriate phrase. That's what I thought you'd called me about. And now you tell me about seeing Ingrid."

"You think they may be linked?" Dag asked him.

Rolf actually frowned. "Who can say, it would be a very strange coincidence."

"Hmm, but as you know, I don't like coincidences. But what about the map? Have you found out anything, the police didn't?"

"We've checked the prints more thoroughly, but have got no further than they had. But, explain to me how you got hold of it. I'd sooner hear it from your own lips than what I read in the police report."

Dag told him. How someone had bumped into him in the train station and had dropped the map, but how they had disappeared into the crowd and down the escalators to the airport train before he could see them properly.

Rolf asked him the exact timings. As Dag told him he typed away on his mobile phone, passing on the information.

"We'll get the security cameras checked." Rolf told Dag. "With knowing the exact time it won't be difficult and we'll be able to trace the suspect back in time and forward. We should then be able to pick them up at the airport. But they could be anywhere in the world by now."

"Not necessarily." Intervened Finn who had been all but forgotten by the other two.

They both looked at him.

"Well," Finn explained himself, "they may not have been going anywhere, they may have been going to pick someone up."

Even Rolf raised an eyebrow. "Hmm, good thinking Finn, we'll have to check both departures and arrivals. And that means the person could still be in Oslo."

"And something could be happening soon." Finn added.

"Yes, exactly." Rolf said. He looked at his watch and rose to go. "I have a meeting, I must get going."

At that moment Finn's phone pinged. Rolf was putting on his coat but waited a moment.

"Kenneth." Finn explained.

Rolf looked at Dag. Dag explained that it was Finn's contact in the City Hall who was finding out if anyone important was visiting in the near future. They had thought it might be relevant.

Rolf turned back to Finn. "And?" He asked.

Finn shook his head. "No-one visiting and nothing of any importance happening in the next couple of weeks."

Rolf nodded. "Good news. Or, bad, depends which way you look at it."

Finn looked at him questioningly, but Rolf ignored him. "By

the way Dag, I've extended your stay at the hotel, hope you don't mind. It's paid for of course. Now, I really must go." He said, turned and left.

"What did he mean, good news, or bad? And he meant that you'll be staying, I suppose?" Finn asked Dag when Rolf had gone.

"Just that it could mean we have nothing to worry about, nothing specific. But, not knowing anything specific means we know nothing at all, which is bad news, whoever is up to whatever they are up to is a blank to us. We have no leads, and that's not good. And as far as my staying here for longer than I expected, yes, I suppose I am."

6.

There was not much Dag could do the next day. He had seen what he'd wanted to see and Finn called to say that his father had wanted him to go through some of his mother's effects and decide what to do with them; he wouldn't take no for an answer. So, Dag was twiddling his thumbs in his hotel room watching increasing sleet from the window drawing a veil over the square and small park outside. He'd put the TV on and the weather forecast was for it to worsen. It was not a day for traipsing around the streets of the city.

He needed to do something. Perhaps a book. He could easily go downstairs and into the station and get one from one of the shops. But he wasn't in the mood for it. He'd probably only end up with a detective novel anyway, and that was the last thing he wanted to delve into.

He wondered if there wasn't anything else he could find out about the Council House, anything that might give a hint as to why someone would be so interested in the security provisions. There just had to be something. No-one would go to so much trouble otherwise.

He sat at the dressing table come desk where his laptop had been left on charge and opened it up. In the background the weather report had change to the rolling news.

He searched again for anything relating to the City Hall over the next couple of weeks and then extended his search to four weeks. There was nothing. He wasn't surprised in a way, he was sure that Finn was better at this than he was.

What if the City Hall was only indirectly connected, he wondered? In that case it was the reason nothing stood out. But what could that be? Someone passing by? A visitor not directly connected to it. It could even be a tourist like himself, albeit someone probably a lot more famous. If so, were there any important or famous people visiting Oslo? Maybe an artist, singer or actor, possibly a foreign dignitary or politician. It would be a substantial list.

As his thoughts grew so did the possibilities until there were too many to make any headway with. He leant back in the chair and stared at the wall.

In the background a news item was droned on about the problems of the world, and a setback in an African country where peace had recently been secured, only now to be put in reverse. The story wafted passed him beyond his awareness. He sighed and decided that he needed a good strong black coffee, and that meant leaving the hotel room. What they provided just wasn't up to scratch and he'd have to search out a nearby decent cafe despite the weather.

He checked out the map on his phone after searching for cafes, which was something that a paper map could not do. He found a likely one just a five minute walk away. Their web page looked like they knew about coffee, proper Baristas and a whole page on the knowledge of different aromas and flavours.

As soon as he walked in he was assailed by the smell of roasting and brewing coffee and was asked in detail what sort of coffee he wanted. It was a little piece of paradise, a warm hug against the outside weather.

He'd bought a newspaper on the way. There was nothing worse than sitting alone in a cafe, to for that matter a bar or restaurant, without anything to occupy you, trying not to stare at customers or servers, ending up staring out of the window for nothing better to do.

He put his coffee to the side of the table and opened out the newspaper. He hadn't bothered with the front page which was taken up with an international news story. What he liked to look for were any of the more interesting but smaller reports, hidden away amongst the other pages. Tales of ordinary lives and, perhaps, crimes, interesting crimes. Although most crimes were, inevitably, as mundane as the lives of the people who committed them. Only rarely was there one which piqued his interest, and then, more often than not, turned out to have an obvious cause. After all, most of the more interesting crimes – murders - were usually carried out between family members, or by people known to the victim. But now and then, just once in a while, something stood out as being different, and that is what he kept his eyes out for.

Today, however, was not to be an interesting day.

He turned the newspaper to the back page. Sport as usual. Folded it and, looking at his now empty cup, signalled for a re-fill.

He looked around the cafe and at the people sat at the tables. As mixed a crowd of metropolitans as one might see in any city cafe. Then, he admonished himself. There he was doing what he so disliked, gazing at the other customers, invading their space. His eyes wandered to the street scene outside.

The server put the now fresh cup of coffee before him and Dag thanked him. He blew on the hot coffee and took a loud sip.

People walked by, some one way, some the other, passing each other within centimetres, but in lives that might be metres or more apart.

It was the colour of the coat that brought Dag from what had become a daydream. It stood out. And the walk. He knew the walk. Her head was covered, and he could not see the face. But he did not need to. He knew who it was. And she was in a hurry again.

He leapt up and grabbed his coat. His hand went to his pocked and he pulled out some money and dropped it onto the table. His newspaper was left behind. He almost ran to the door. He got his coat on just as he exited the cafe. He looked down the street, the way that she had gone and saw here covered head bobbing in the crowd some way in the distance. He walked fast. On the outside of the pavement stepping into the road to get past people. But the snow was coming down harder and it was difficult to keep her in sight.

It was only two blocks along Prinsens Gate, heading

towards the Station, when she suddenly crossed the road and into a side road; Fred Olsenes Gate. Dag was stopped at the crossing by slow moving cars and, against the usual obedience of what the Americans would call jaywalking, acted like a policeman and ran between the cars to the blare of horns.

She was gaining ground on him. The snow was now coming down in great wet flakes, but he still caught of her brightly coloured headgear in the distance. He sped up, almost to a run.

She crossed another busy interchange, and again Dag was held up and the as much as the distance between them had narrowed it widened again. He ran now and bumped into people generating protests and some swearwords. As he ran he slipped and then slid on the pavement. He had not worn shoes suitable for a chase in these circumstances.

Only a hundred or so metres ahead was another large, wide crossroads. She was still at least fifty metres or more ahead of him. She reached the crossroads and Dag expected her to pause and cross. Then he could close the gap.

Suddenly she was gone, hidden by a sudden sheet of falling snow. It cleared. She wasn't at the crossing, nor could Dag see her on it. He ran to the edge of the road at the crossing. He looked over to the other side but couldn't see her. He looked right; nothing. He looked left. There was her coat. She was along the road to the left.

But Dag almost swore. She was getting onto a bus. She disappeared onto it. Dag ran, slipping and sliding on the wet snowing surface. The bus's indicator flashed, It was pulling out. The doors had closed. Dag reach the rear of the bus as it was pulling out into the traffic.

He stopped and caught his breath. He noted the bus's number – 17.

Ingrid had done it again. Escaped him.

Dag checked the timetable in the bus shelter. It was a long bus route. In the direction she was travelling it went all the way out to Oslo University Hospital and just beyond, about four kilometers away. She could be going almost anywhere.

His breathing recovered he took out his phone and called Rolf's number. Again there was no reply, so he would have to wait.

He was now wet, cold, and miserable. He needed another coffee, There was probably nowhere better than the cafe, so despite having to walk all the way back, he retraced his steps.

He took the same seat, his newspaper still folded up upon it. The server brought him the correct coffee without him asking. The server smiled but was accompanied by a sideways look as he walked away.

He sat, looking out of the window. He'd sooner not have but it helped him think. Not that any answers came into his mind, only questions. He could only make wild guesses as to why Ingrid was here in Oslo – if she had ever been away since they had last encountered one another. But it was a question for Rolf and his department. Why Dag was remaining in Oslo was because of the map. However, Dag also knew that it would continue to trouble him. It was a coincidence, that was for sure, and that was what Dag didn't like about it. He didn't like coincidences, for in his time with the police there was almost never a coincidence that was simply such.

Dag's phone pinged and brought him back to the reality of the cafe and the noise of its customers and the clinking of spoons against crockery.

There was no name and he didn't recognise the number. He read it.

'Stay at the cafe, I will be there in ten minutes. Randi.'

Randi? He certainly knew no woman called Randi. Then he thought of the initial letter. It was R. He knew enough about Rolf and his organisation to know that all their operatives, at least the one's he'd met, used the letter for their pseudonym. He had to assume that she was an E14 agent. If not, then he would have to be very careful. But. Who else could have found out so easily where he was. He wondered if he was being tailed, it was entirely possible. Or, perhaps, they were monitoring his mobile phone signal. He would have to wait to find out.

As he waited his phone pinged again. This time it was Finn asking if he had heard any news about the map. He replied to say he hadn't but would call him that evening as he might soon find out something.

The last few minutes ticked slowly by, and then, on the stroke of ten minutes the door opened and in walked a woman. Her eyes alighted immediately ion Dag and she strode over. She was not what Dag was expecting. Somehow or other he had expected to be confronted with a sort of James Bond partner; leggy, blond, feline. But here was a woman, probably in her forties, dressed as a rather mature, tortoise-shell spectacle -wearing, secretary, from a old-fashioned firm of solicitors. Nothing like the agent he expected. But, maybe, she wasn't, maybe she was someone entirely different.

She wasn't. She sat down without being invited and introduced herself simply as Randi, no surname, and covertly showed him her ID. She did not smile.

"Mr Meldel." She began. "Rolf has assigned me to you."

"My minder?" Dag asked, trying to say it jokily, but making sound rather sarcastic. The, feeling himself blush slightly as she gave him an frosty stare.

"Liaison officer." She corrected him.

"Of course. Well, have you got any news for me?"

She went quiet as the server asked if she wanted anything, and she ordered a tea; if they did lemon tea. He said they would be able to, and retreated.

Randi glanced behind Dag where a mirror hung. Dag realised then that when she had come in and taken her seat she had moved it slightly to one side so that she could use the view from it. She was not the simple secretary that she appeared to be, she was well trained.

Satisfied, she continued. "We have identified the person who collided with you. She did not go straight to departures but went to arrivals, as I believe your nephew suggested. There she met a man. We were unable to overhear their conversation. From there she went to departures and flew out of the country."

Randi stopped as the server brought her the lemon tea. She had paused before he came having spotted him in the mirror.

"And you know where she went and who she met?" Dag

asked hoping to prise the information from her rather than her leaving it at that.

"Yes, she took a flight to Copenhagen. Our colleagues in Denmark are keeping an eye on her. And as far as the man she met; he is a newly posted Defence attaché to a foreign embassy."

"And what exactly is she doing in Copenhagen?" Dag asked.

Randi's eyes flicked to the mirror again and after a second's hesitation continued. Dag was facing the other way and could see all that was happening in the cafe and could not see anything to warrant her awareness.

"She has a position at an embassy there, but not the same country as our new friend here."

"You haven't mention which countries are involved here."

"Rolf has told me that you can be told the nationality of the new defence attaché. He is from Ikebaje. His name is Brigadier Malidi Jata. He is the brother-in-law of their president."

The name meant nothing to Dag, although he vaguely recalled hearing the name of the country.

"So, what now?" Dag asked.

"So, that is all for now. Will will keep in regular contact – say at 11:00 hrs and 19:00 hrs each day. I will use this phone." Randi held the phone she had with her. It was a simple pre-paid one which could not be easily traced. She sent a text and Dag's phone pinged immediately. "There, you have my number."

"That's not quite everything though is it?" Dag queried.

This time Randi half raised an eyebrow. "There is something else?"

"Yes, the reason I tried to contact Rolf an hour or so back."

"You did?"

"Actually, I thought that's why we were meeting, so I could tell you why I was trying to call him."

Randi quickly realised what it might be. "Ah, you mean Ingrid. Why? Have you thought of something else that you forgot to mention earlier?"

Dag sighed. "No, I'd not forgotten anything."

"Then why .." Randi began and Dag held a finger up.

"I've seen her again, that's why. No more than an hour ago."

Dag told her what had happened, his chase after Ingrid and her escape.

"It was a number 17 bus." He told her.

Randi had taken another phone from her pocket and was texting as he spoke.

"I've passed that on. Most interesting. Just a coincidence though, I would think." She looked Dag in the eyes. "But you don't believe in coincidences , so Rolf says."

"They happen. I'm sure about that. But I don't like them, no.

By the way, what about Finn, my nephew, he's going to ask questions. He knows everything that's gone on so far."

Randi was standing up and putting her coat on to leave.

"Ah, yes, Finn. Rolf says he has no objection to his involvement. You may tell him as much as you think he needs to know."

"He hasn't signed anything. So, how much does he need to know?"

Randi shrugged. "Rolf seems happy for him to be involved, so how much is up to you. Now I must go. Remember, 11:00 and 19:00 ."

Dag watched her go, finished his coffee and paid the bill – for himself and Randi. The snow has eased off and he walked back to the hotel. He decided on a nice hot bath for once instead of a shower and lay back and luxuriated in it.

Afterwards, in a soft white dressing gown, he lay on his bed and called Finn.

"I'm glad you called Uncle Dag. I can't take much more of dad. He's getting rid of everything that mum loved. It's as if he's wiping her from our memory. I just don't get it."

"Well, let's meet up tomorrow. We can talk about it then. It must be hard for him to cope with I suppose."

"It's hard for me and Anette as well, Does he think it's just him."

"It's hard for you all I'm sure. But let's talk about it tomorrow, when we're together."

"OK." Finn reluctantly agreed, then brightened. "Have you got any info yet on the map? Or that woman?"

"I've heard something, yes. But let's go over that tomorrow as well; not on the phone."

"Oh, right, yes, of course. What time shall I come?"

"How about I buy us breakfast. I fancy a change from the hotel's. What time can you get here?"

"I'll be there as early as you want. How about eight -thirty?"

"OK, eight-thirty it is."

In the background the TV had been droning on. Dag hadn't taken any notice of it, it was the news channel again. Why he had it on when he didn't listen to what they were talking about he didn't know. As he thought about Finn and his father, and Anders' strange attitude to his wife's memory, or rather those things that made up her memories, the news item passed him by; he had not heard the name of the country the report featured.

He lay in bed, in the dark. Well, the not-quite-so-dark. The hotel curtains were not thick enough to keep out all of the light from the city. He unused to it. At home his bedroom face the dark emptiness if the North Sea with only the stars and maybe the moon for illumination when the clouds failed to blanket the sky. Here it was more difficult to get to sleep. But it wasn't only the light.

He had come to Oslo to attend his sister's funeral, that was all. And now even that did not seem the simple matter that it should have been. Then, of course, he had, through no fault of his ow, purely by accident, had to contact the police about the map. If only he had not been so inquisitive or suspicious; if only his past had not stayed with him, he might have thrown it away and forgotten about it. And then, there was matter of Ingrid. A coincidence that again forced him to connect with Rolf and his people. He had not wanted or even expected in his wildest imagination that such a coincidence might occur. But it had.

And now he was tied, tied to events, events that had carried him along with them, against his will. He had thought he'd left all of that behind. But no, the fates were against that. What annoyed him most was that he had not resisted, he had allowed himself to be swept along with events. He had just gone with the flow. At each point he could have ignored them, he could have simply carried on with his new mundane existence. But that was it, a boring, mundane existence. That was why he had not resisted or refused, or raised a word or thought against his involvement.

But where was his involvement taking him? How far down this path would he go? And, he must not forget Finn. Somehow or other he was taking Finn with him.

Finn, though, was part the whole. Anders and the reason for his sister's death, a death which, according to Finn's words, may have been avoidable. It was another path that stood before him, and he had to decide if he should take it. Maybe, he should just let sleeping dogs lie. After all there was no evidence that Anders directly caused Kristine's death, just that he may have delayed her diagnosis, and that was not an offence. A contributory factor, yes, but not strictly an offence. Unless, of course, there was a motive behind it. If there was, Dag would not be able to let the dogs lie.

Finally even his whirring thoughts could keep him awake any longer and one moment he was awake, and the next asleep.

7.

It was still dark when Dag woke, but then, it would still be dark when Finn came. It would be another half an hour before the sun brought daylight and, even then, it would only be bright if the clouds had cleared.

Dag had a very quick shower. He felt like he hardly needed one after the long soak in the bath the previous, but it was habit of course. He was downstairs in the lobby by twenty past eight. The clouds had cleared and the snow had changed to rain during the early hours removing its covering from the street.

Dag had checked out which cafes were open for breakfast on his phone and the nearest, and best looking one, was just a minute or so walk away. They served everything from a simple yoghurt and granola concoction to a full American. He guessed which one Finn would choose, and knew that for himself the granola would be out. He had not yet taken his pills and would have to take them once he'd eaten in the cafe.

Finn arrived bang on time, and they set off straight away for the cafe. As they walked Finn began to ask questions but Dag told him to wait until they were sitting comfortably having breakfast.

To Dag's surprise Finn didn't go for the American breakfast selection but instead chose the smoked salmon with scrambled eggs on sourdough bread. Dag, feeling he should take the youngsters example and restrain himself, changed his mind and ordered the same with, of course, strong black coffee; Finn had freshly squeezed orange juice.

When the food and drinks had been delivered Finn was keen to get answers.

Dag told him that Rolf had sent him a liaison officer whose name was Randi. Finn smiled and Dag gave him one of his police stares. Finn said sorry. Dag told him that the person he had bumped into had been traced on the cameras, and that Finn had been correct; she – for it was a woman – had met someone at the airport, but then had gone to departures and flown to Copenhagen.

"That's a bit suspicious isn't it?" Finn pointed out.

"A bit, yes. And on top of that, she works for an embassy there – and before you ask, no I wasn't told which one."

"Oh." Finn looked disappointed. "Do they know who she met?" he asked more brightly.

"Yes. A man taking up a post as a defence attaché at another embassy – not the country she works for evidently." Dag told him.

"Even more suspicious, surely?"

Dag gave a half shrug. "Not necessarily. I believe both countries may be close to each other – African Randi said. So, it might be natural that they work together in different ways. But, odd enough for Rolf and his people to keep an eye on them."

"But then, what does the map mean? Maybe, she was going to pass it to him?"

Again Dag shrugged. "Why? There's nothing on it that couldn't be found out easily by either embassy."

"Hmm." Finn mused, then said. "What if their embassies don't know that they were meeting and about the map?"

Dag put down the coffee cup he'd just taken a sip from. "That they might be working independently, or at least one or other of them is acting against their own embassy? Hmm, that's a good point, but it certainly complicates things. Not that we are necessarily going to get any more involved in things anyway."

"We're not?" Finn said in surprise. "But, I thought we were, sort of, part of things, part of the investigation."

Dag smiled. "I doubt that very much. I happened on something and passed it to them, that's all. We have helped them, but it doesn't mean that we're going to have any further involvement."

"Oh." Finn said, his enthusiasm punctured. "You mean we might not hear anything else."

"Not unless they consider it absolutely necessary, no."

Finn was silent for a while whilst he finished off his food. When he finished he leaned forward and asked. "What about that other woman? What about her? She can't be involved in this map, she's another case. Maybe they'll want you to track her?"

Dag smiled. "I think they are perfectly capable of tracking her down without me."

"Oh. So that's it. Is it."

"I'm afraid you career as a detective may prove to be short-lived, Finn."

"Then there's nothing for it, I'll have to join the force."

"Your father won't stop you then?" Dag asked as a way of coming around to the problems between Finn and his father.

Finn shook his head rather miserably. "I can't understand him, don't know why he's getting rid of all the things mum liked the most. He just won't let us keep them."

"Is Anette upset as well?"

Finn nodded. "She was dad's favourite, but even she doesn't understand what he's doing."

"Perhaps he blames himself in some way. By getting rid of things that remind him of her he is somehow trying to draw a line under that blame. If those things that remind him of her aren't there, then he feels he can clear his mind of any blame or responsibility. Though, surely, it was sudden and no-one could have prevented it, so he shouldn't be blaming himself at all?"

Finn's face became dark. "I'm not so sure. I think mum knew something was wrong for some time, but dad just kept saying she was being silly, stupid. I think he stopped her going to the doctors to find out."

Dag felt a sudden shiver. What Finn said had flicked a switch in his detective's mind. He had heard too many statements like that in the past for one not to cause him a twinge of anxiety.

"But she did go?" Dag asked.

"Only after, I don't know, maybe months."

"I'm sure your father was just saying it so that she wouldn't be worrying, that he really thought she was OK. And now he's blaming himself. We all make mistakes you know. And sometimes they have worse consequences than we can ever foresee." Dag told him, but inwardly he had doubts. What if his sister's death was, in some way, Anders' fault after all?

Before he could say anything else, his phone pinged. It wasn't yet 11:00 but it was a message from Randi.

"Who is it from?" Finn asked as Dag read it.

It was only a short message. Dag looked up. "It's from Randi, she wants us to meet."

"Can I come?"

Dag almost said 'no', but he remembered that Rolf, for his own reasons, had said that he had no objection to Finn being involved, and besides that, Dag liked his company, and the thoughts he came up with.

"Yes. Rolf said it would be OK, and I'd like you to be present."

A wide smile wiped away the gloom from Finn's face.

"Great!" he said. "Where do we go?"

"Nowhere." Said Dag. "She'll be here shortly."

Dag was even more sure that his phone was being tracked. He didn't like it. If he was only reporting the map to them, if he was only passing on to them the sighting of Ingrid, why were they taking so much care to keep him under observation.

Randi appeared just five minutes later. She came directly to their table and adjusted a seat to join them. This time making sure she had a clear view of the room as well as the street outside.

"Mr Meldel." She nodded to him. Dag had so far not bothered to tell her to call him Dag and left her to talk to him formally. "And you must be Finn." She gave Finn an intense look.

It made Finn uneasy, but with the blaséness of youth just replied, "Hi."

"So," Asked Dag, "to what do we owe this honour?"

Randi looked at him blankly clearly unimpressed by his

expression.

"Rolf has asked me to ask you if you might do him a favour."

Dag wasn't keen on the word favour, and he wasn't keen that Rolf was using Randi to request it.

"I've been thinking about things." Dag began. "I have passed information on to you, but in no way have I agreed to do anything more. I'm no longer a detective, after all, and don't have any authority to get actively involved in whatever investigations my small bit of evidence may have initiated."

Dag could see from the corner of his eye that Finn had looked at him and frowned.

"You are under no obligation at all, that is true. But, knowing your reputation, I would not have thought that, if you could help, you would refuse to do so. After all, your country may depend upon it, and despite your condition Rolf was sure that you wouldn't let us down. One might use the word duty, but that would seem like we were pressing you to help us. He'd much prefer it if you agreed to help without any pressure."

Dag let her statement hang in the air for a moment. "No pressure then." He sighed and gave a chuckle. "All right, I'll help. But I'm not sure about involving Finn."

"I'll help, of course I will!" Finn exclaimed, replying for himself.

"There, you see how keen he is." said Randi. "You'll have to keep him in check."

Dag sighed. He knew he must go along with the flow of events. "So, what is it he wants us to do."

"Nothing covert, obviously. And we have people who can track people on the ground. In fact, we believe we have tracked someone, you friend and ours, Ingrid."

"Ah. Well, that's good news." Dag surmised.

"Yes, we're keeping an eye on her, of course. But, we would like to give her a prod; see what she does and where she goes, without giving away our own interest in her." Randi paused.

"Hmm, so that's where we come, in is it?" Dag guessed.

"I imagine she will recognise you. She's not likely to have forgotten you. But she won't necessarily thing that you are currently directly linked to our department. If she sees you she is likely to make some sort of move and we can track it."

"And how do you intend to let her see me?"

"We have traced her to a French restaurant where she is apparently working as a waitress. It would be quite a natural thing for you to take your nephew for a meal whilst you are here in Oslo; or rather another meal. But, we want her to recognise you, not for you to recognise her. You must act as if you have never seen her before. It shouldn't be too difficult. After all many people bother taking notice of their servers. Very few, unless they are attracted to them. And that would mean that Finn, you must act as if she doesn't exist, even if you are attracted to her, which is entirely possible for a young man of your age."

"I think I can manage to act that part." Finn said with a

little indignation. "I was pretty good in the school plays."

"In parts where you were meant to sweep a young girl off her feet no doubt." Randi countered.

Dag spoke to stop the interaction between the two. "And where do we find her?"

"At this brasserie." Randi told him passing over a business card. "It's not too far away, on Øvre Slottsgate. "we've made a booking for you in your name, for two people, for eight-thirty this evening. We left it a bit later as it will probably be busier. We didn't want you turning up when he place was half empty. Full, it will be easier for you to ignore her, or she you if she spots you and wants to avoid you."

Dag looked at the business card. "Is it expensive?" He asked.

Randi gave a short sigh. "You may keep the receipts and I'll pas them on to accounts as expenses."

Dag smiled. He wondered how long it would take for him to receive the repayment.

"Very well." He said. "We'll be there."

Finn didn't go home. He spent the intervening time in Dag's hotel room and made use of the facilities, including the mini-bar so Dag found out later. They left the hotel at 20:15. The restaurant was only a five minute walk away so they'd be there ten minutes before their booking.

The brasserie was surprisingly busy and not the sort of restaurant Dag normally chose; French and expensive. They were taken to their table by a young man, every inch the University student, and were presented with the menus.

They both picked up their copy and Dag looked as surreptitiously as he could over the upper edge of his to see if he could spot Ingrid.

She was there, at the bar, picking up an a tray of drinks for one of the tables.

"Remember, don't take any notice of the servers." Dag reminded Finn.

"Have you seen her? Is she here?" Finn asked.

"Yes, but don't look! She's serving a table with drinks."

From the very edge of his vision Dag tried to keep her in sight whilst he appeared to read the menu. She had deposited the drinks on the customers table and started towards them. Dag looked up at Finn to ask him what he fancied and so that she might see his face more fully. She did. As Dag looked back at the menu he could just catch her coming to a stop, standing still for a second, and then changing her direction. She had turned and headed back to the bar. The server who had given them the menus said something to her and, putting her hand to her head, she answered. Then, she headed for the kitchen serving door.

"She spotted me all right." Dag told Finn.

"She's made some excuse and gone into the kitchen doors. Probably said she wasn't feeling well. That's probably the easiest undercover job I've ever had to do. Now we can just sit back and enjoy an expensive meal at their expense. They can take it from here."

They chose the set menu. A starter of mushrooms, Jerusalem artichokes and poached eggs on a choux pastry, followed by roast duck breast, a sauté of sprouts, potato purée and a truffle sauce. Dag couldn't manage a dessert but Finn polished off a crème brûlée.

They sat back after an hour and a half of eating fully replete.

It was gone ten and most the the customers had now left.

"Come on time to go." Dag said. "You won't be able to get back home now I suppose. I'll see if they've got a spare room at the hotel. You can stay there the night."

"I should still have time to get the last bus." Finn told him.

Dag looked at his watch again. "No, I'll pay. You never know we may get news about tonight's little performance. It;'ll save you coming backwards and forwards. And anyway, I was thinking I might go back with you tomorrow. I'd like a chance to talk to your dad."

"Oh, don't tell him I said anything, please!" Finn implored him.

"I think I can managed to be discreet. I'll say I just wanted a keepsake, something of my sister's to remind me of her."

"Oh, OK then." Finn said unconvincingly.

They had exited the restaurant and turned left. It was about a ten minute walk back to the hotel. This part of Oslo had been pedestrianised as a shopping centre. They walked through the now almost deserted shopping street until they reached a vehicular road and turned left again. There was practically no traffic and even the parking spaces were nearly all empty. The straight road would take them all the way to square in front of the hotel to the side of the Railway Station.

The purr of the car in the distance heading towards them, its headlights on, but not on full beam, was not out of place. It drove down the road as any car would have done. Few people were about and Dag and Finn were all but the only ones on their stretch of pavement. The car slowed as if looking at a parking space or trying to find a side street of which there was none. Dag and Finn took no notice and talked about how Dag should handle Finn's father. The car drew closer.

Dag's ears had been attuned to sounds that did not fit in to their surroundings, but in the space of time since his retirement his senses had perhaps dulled partially. The purr of the engine altered. Its revs accelerated. It did so even though the car slowed imperceptibly as if a feline about to leap onto its prey. Dag checked his step. Finn walked a couple of steps ahead of him.

Then, the engine roared. The cat-like car leapt forward. Its lights blazed into full beam blinding Dag. His arm reached out for Finn but touched the air.

"Watch out!" He screamed. "Finn!"

The car made a screeching sound and there was a thump as it hit the curb. It was upon them in a couple of seconds. Its tyres screamed as they bit the pavement.

Dag shouted again. "Finn!" Then he dived to his side, and luckily into a shop doorway.

He heard another thump and crash as the car hit the side of the shop and then careered back onto the road. Dag was on the ground huddled up against the shop door. He breathed heavily, then shouted for Finn again.

He pushed himself up onto his feet and glanced quickly at the disappearing car, then turned quickly to look for Finn. His heart was in his mouth. The road and pavement was empty. He looked down at the tyre marks. He looked fro blood. There was none.

He called out again. "Finn!"

"Here! Here, uncle Dag." Came his voice. Then, an ashen face appeared out of the next doorway.

Dag ran to him. "Are you hurt? Did it get you?"

"No, no, I'm all right. I thought it had got you. I think I was a bit quicker than you getting out of the way."

They both took deep breaths and leaned against the shop front. The shop alarm had began ringing. The police would soon be there. Dag didn't wait for them to turn up, he sent Randi a text and marked it URGENT. He hoped she would get there before the police. There would be some explaining to do.

"I'm sorry, we hadn't thought there would such an immediate response." Randi apologised. "She must have made a call from the restaurant staff room. Unfortunately she left early saying she was ill and then she gave us the slip. We've got her apartment under surveillance though, and she's not turned up there yet."

"If she does." said Dag. "She's always been pretty good at disappearing – must have contingency plans in place."

"

Yes, you may be right. I'll keep you informed, but for now you'd both better get some rest."

They were back at the hotel. They had made sure Finn had a room for the night. It was certainly safer than making his way home. Randi told them that someone would be on duty there, just to be on the safe side. Finn sat on the side of Dag's bed drinking a mug of hot sweet coffee when Randi left them. Despite the heat of the coffee and the warmth of the room Finn began to shiver and then shake. Dag sat beside him and out his hands upon his shoulders, rubbed them, and then put a blanket around him.

"I think you need to have a hot bath. You're suffering from shock."

8.

Dag left Finn sleeping until nearly ten then knocked on his door. Finn was up and opened it.

"Did you told your father anything?" Dag asked.

"No. I called him but just said I was staying in town. I sometimes stay with a friend. He doesn't worry if I don't go home."

"Well, you must have something to eat, and then we'll go back to your home. You can't wear those clothes forever."

"Are you going to talk to him?" Finn asked.

"Like I said, I'll be discreet. I don't want to antagonise him, he'll only clam up if I do, and probably lose his temper. If I remember rightly, he could be pretty touchy at the best of times."

After Finn had eaten at a cafe in the railway station, they caught the train to Slependen station. Finn lived at the end of a small terrace of houses just a five-minute walk from the station.

Finn went in and Dag stood just inside in the doorway once the door was shut. Finn called out to say it was him. It was Anette who came from the kitchen to ask where he had been, then stopped short when she saw Dag.

She looked from Dag to Finn, and gave Finn a close look.

"What's wrong. You don't look well. Has something happened? You didn't come home last night, I was worried."

"It's nice to know you were. I don't suppose dad did."

"That's not fair." She then said to Dag, "I'm sorry uncle Dag, come in, don't just stand there."

"Thank you. Is your father in?"

"No. What is it? Something has happened hasn't it." Anette replied.

"It's nothing we were nearly hit by a car last night. We gad a close call, had to jump out of the way. The police suspect a drunken driver."

"You weren't hurt though?" Anette asked.

"No we're fine." Dag reassured her. "You said your father was out. Will he be back any time soon?"

"I don't know, he didn't say."

Anette was younger than Finn by two years. Even so, Dag thought that her father should at least say where he was going. Although, with mobile phones these days he supposed that Anders would on;y be a call away if necessary.

"Oh, well, never mind. I just thought we could have a chat, that's all." Dag told her.

"What about?" Anette frowned.

"I just wondered how he was getting on. It can't be easy for him."

"What have you been saying?" Anette turned on Finn. "What stories have you been telling."

"Anette!" Dag said assertively. "Finn has not been telling tales of any sort. He was just worried about your father. Concerned about how he was reacting to your mothers death."

Anette's eyes narrowed. "He's been saying things about father. There's nothing wrong with him. He just wants to start a new life. He wants to put the old one behind him, that's all. Why should he live in the past? It's over. Mother's gone. Finn just needs to accept it. And why do you think you can interfere anyway? What did you ever do for her; or us. I don't remember ever seen you since we were born. What has this got to do with you?"

She was right about that, at least. He had little right to turn up and intervene in their lives. But what Finn had said about his sister not seeing a doctor earlier concerned him. He decided to be blunt.

"You are correct in a way, I have little right to interfere. But I do have some right, no matter how small. Your mother was my sister and that gives me at least some right. I will be blunt. I am concerned that she wasn't allowed to see any doctors sooner than she did, that she may have been prevented from doing so."

"How dare you!" Anette almost screamed. "Father would never have hurt her."

"So," Said Dag. "You know who a meant. I hadn't mentioned your father."

"He didn't think it was necessary that's all. Mum was fine she didn't need a doctor."

"But she did, didn't she?"

"It's you!" Anette pointed at Finn. "You're the one spreading these lies!"

"He was worried, concerned, that's all." Dag tried to say, but Anette began to scream.

"Get out! Get out!" Both of you! Don't come back. I'm going to tell father and he won't let you back." She shouted at Finn.

Finn had been white-faced throughout, but then he held himself straight and said quietly, "I'll get my things. Don't worry I'll not come back."

"No wait ..." Dag began, but Anette, red-faced, turned about, stomped into the kitchen and slammed the door behind her.

Dag let out a deep breath. "That went well. You'd better get your things, Finn. She'll calm down I'm sure."

Finn just nodded and went upstairs.

Dag was cursing himself. He had never handled a situation like that so badly. He certainly had lost his touch. Anette could clearly not see her father in a bad light, and Dag didn't think he was going to change it. And there was no evidence of any sort to point the finger directly at Anders as having worsened his sister's condition. Suspicion, yes. But nothing concrete and nothing to suggest that it was intentional. He may just have a thing against doctors, hospitals, medical science; people do, especially some religious groups. Maybe that was it. Was Anders a member of some religious cult? Finn had not mentioned it.

One person would have more information about Kristine's condition; her doctor. But he would not be able to speak to Dag, unless Dag was a detective, which he no longer was.

Finn came downstairs with a large bag.

"Are you sure?" Dag asked him.

Finn nodded. "I can't stay here, not now."

"Will you tell Anette you're leaving? It would be best. You shouldn't leave without a word."

Finn though a moment and then nodded. He went to the kitchen door. "Anette? I'm leaving."

 There was silence.

"I'm going now." He listened. He heard a muffled noise, it

sounded like crying. "Please don't let me leave without saying something, Anette."

All he heard was the clattering of the kettle being filled.

"You know my number. If you want to call me you can. Any time." Finn added.

There was no reply so he turned and said, "Come on, let's go."

Once outside, Dag said. "I'm afraid that was my fault. I handled it really badly. I should have known better."

Finn shook his head. "No. You're not to blame. It was coming to that anyway."

They walked back to the station. They were silent for most of the way but once on the platform Dag asked him, "Is your father part of any religious group?"

Finn was staring at the railway track and didn't look up. "Oh that. All the religion stuff. I think that's what started it. Dad tried to get me involved. That's when we really started falling out. Mum just went along with it I think, just to please him. Now he's got Anette into it."

"Why didn't you tell me before?"

Finn looked up. "Is it important?"

"It may be. I've come across groups like this before. They have beliefs which are, how should I say, against prevailing science, and I think, wisdom. But enough of that for now. What are you going to do. I don't expect you've thought through any plans?"

"Well, we're still helping the government, aren't we? I thought I could stay at the hotel for a while while I help you."

"And who do you think will be paying for that?"

"I thought your government friends might do. They're paying for you after all, aren't they?"

"I'm not sure they'll want us for anything else now, not since that attempt on our lives. They'll want us out the way."

"Attempt on our lives." Finn said slowly. "I hadn't sort of thought of it like that, but it was, wasn't it? But what about the map? There's still the matter of the map."

Dag shrugged. "I'm sure they can follow that up. I can't see that they'll need us in conjunction with that."

Finn looked disappointed. But the train came and they finished the conversation. Dag tried to get off the subject on the ride back into the city, but his mind was busy. The thoughts about Anders and the group he now belonged to, the effect it might be having on his niece, the recalling of the car attack, and a sneaking concern that what he had said to Finn about not being needed in the matter of the map, preyed on his mind. Somehow or other he didn't think that any of them were over. None had come to their end, all had life still left in them.

9.

"And when your stay here comes to an end, what then?" Dag asked Finn.

Outside of the hotel's few comfortable chairs, the coffee lounge area was fairly utilitarian. Dag and Finn had walked to the cafe he had found before which served coffee acceptable to his discerning taste.

"Um, well I thought, maybe, I thought that I might come to Kristiansund for a bit. I mean, just so I found my feet. You now, made up my mind about things; about what I wanted to do and that." Finn sort of explained.

Dag sighed, but he wasn't surprised. He had more than half expected the answer, and he wasn't sure that he could find the words to put him off the idea.

"What about your sister? What if she needs help? Surely it would be better for you to stay close to her?" Dag asked him.

"You don't want me. Is that what you're trying to say? Please don't put my sister on me. She's got her own mind, she can decide what she wants to do."

"Maybe she can, maybe she can't. Those, for the better word, sects, can control people's minds, you know. And no, I'm not saying I don't want you coming to Kristiansund. I just want you to be absolutely sure, that's all."

"So, I can come to Kristiansund?" Finn looked hopefully at Dag.

"If you are absolutely sure. But we are not going to make a decision today. We'll stay at the hotel for a few more days and then decide. It'll give me chance to make some investigations about this group your father belongs to." Dag told him. And he also wanted to get to speak to his sister's doctor if he could.

Finn smiled and his eyes lit up. "I won't change my mind. I never do, not once I've made it up."

Dag could believe that.

Dag had bought a newspaper and it lay on the table between them, but he had not looked at it. He preferred to read when he was alone and not being interrupted or sidetracked by anyone. It was folded showing the bottom half of the front page, but was turned away from him and faced Finn. Finn looked at it and began reading one of the main article at the bottom of the page.

Then, he picked it up and read the whole article. Dag wondered what had attracted his interest.

"Something interesting?" Dag asked.

"There's a story here. It's about a guy at the Ikebage Embassy. A Brigadier; Malidi Shomari Jata. He's just arrived. He's their defence attaché. Brother-in-law to the president. Didn't Randi say something about the man the woman met at the airport being that? It must be him."

"Let me see." Dag asked.

"The president's the guy getting the Nobel Peace Prize this year. It'll be next month." Finn added.

Dag read the article. He was named in relation to the deteriorating peace, or what was peace, in Ikebage. He had been in charge of a Regiment that some say had committed an atrocity, but he argued that it was the fault of the Colonel directly in charge and that the man had been arrested and charged with incompetence. His hands, he declared, were clean. But the fact was that the man awarded the Peace Prize was the President and the worsening situation between the ethnic tribes and religions was drawing a cloud over the Prize.

'And not for the first time.' Dag thought.

"And if that map has something to do with him?" Finn suggested. "It's important, isn't it?"

Dag gave a node and put the newspaper down. "I'm pretty sure that link must have already been looked into. They'll be keeping a close eye on him."

"But, why were the marks on the map of the City Hall?" Finn pondered allowed.

"Isn't that where the prize is given out?" Dag said, now taking more interest.

"It was, yes. But since they did it at the University last year, I think they're doing it there again this year."

"So the marks on the map don't link the City hall with the Prize-giving? But it always used to be there didn't it?"

"It always was before. The King, Queen, and everyone important goes along."

"Hmm." Mused Dag. "Randi said that the woman was from a different African Embassy in Copenhagen. I wonder which country it was? She didn't say."

"Sounds fishy to me. We should investigate."

"No we shouldn't. That's not our job. You've already seen how dangerous it can be, getting too involved. I lost one of my policewomen once. I'm not going to lose anyone else; most especially you."

"Oh." Finn said, his face clearing of its cheerfulness. "I'm sorry."

"If we are needed they'll let us know. But I think our lives will be a little quieter from now on."

But no sooner had Dag said the words than his phone pinged. It was 11:00 and it was his contact text with Randi.

He read the message. 'Meet me 12:00. Outside City Hall in courtyard.'

"Shit." Dag muttered. "I spoke too soon."

Dag showed Finn the message.

Finn brightened again. "They've got a task for us!"

"Please, don't be so enthusiastic." Dag admonished him.

"Sorry."

Dag looked at the time on his phone. It was 11:20. Then, he looked at the map of Oslo. "It's not far. We've plenty of time."

"I wonder what she wants?" Finn wondered, looking beyond Dag to the street outside.

They walked into the courtyard area with its central fountain and statue of two swans in a strange ritual. Dag looked around. He could not see Randi. But then, he saw Rolf walk out of the shadows under one of the walkways directly where a security camera was positioned.

"I thought we were meeting Randi." Dag said.

"She was unavoidable detained elsewhere. I wasn't far away so came myself." Rolf told him.

"So, what is all this about?" asked Dag.

"A few developments I thought we'd discuss with you. Shall

we have a coffee at that bar on the corner?" Rolf asked.

They went back to to same bar on the corner of the piazza. Rolf said nothing more until they were seated and had their coffees in front of them, and the server had gone back behind the counter.

"Well," said Dag, what's all this about?"

"The first interesting point is that the woman whose map you found did not go to Copenhagen as we thought. I should have learned from your previous cases. She went to departures, of course, and booked in at the desk, but, as it turns out, did not board the plane. Our friends in Denmark alerted us and confirmed it. We then re-checked the camera footage. She returned to Oslo. But, she does not appear to be at her country's embassy. We are trying to trace her."

"So, she's somewhere in Oslo." Dag frowned. "Do you think she's looking for her map. Surely she thinks it must have ended up in the station's waste?"

"One would have thought so." Rolf agreed, but hesitantly.

"One would have?" Dag queried. "That doesn't sound very definite."

"Hmm. A member of the station staff remembers someone – a woman – asking questions on the entrance to platform 10, sometime later. She said she had lost something, and had they noticed anyone picking up a document. They didn't, of course."

"So, she's here looking for her map. But she has no hope of tying me to it, does she?"

"One would have thought not." Rolf replied, meaning the opposite.

"There was another man with her. We went back and checked the security footage. He was there to see her off when she went for the train and bumped into you. It is possible that he saw you and noticed that you picked something up. In which case she was asking questions just to clarify their suspicions."

Dag's heart sank a little. "So, you're saying that they may have a description of me, and might have guessed that I have the map. But they'd hardly be likely to guess where I'm staying."

"Not unless they produced a photofit and began asking questions of the hotels, no."

"Dear god, that's what you think they've done. They know what I look like and they're out there looking for me." Dag moaned.

"Hang on a minute!" Finn interrupted. "It wasn't them who drove that car at us was it?"

Dag looked to Finn and then back to Rolf, his face a gloomy as he could make it. "What do you know?" He asked Rolf.

Rolf took a sip of his coffee and cleared his throat. "We've trace the car. It was hired. The hirer used a false name and documents, of course. But he was black and had a pronounced accent. So, yes, I no longer think it was linked to Ingrid. It looks like it was our friends at the station."

Dag was feeling angry. "Do you think they've traced us to the hotel?"

"Don't worry, we've increased our observation team. You are under the closest watch from now on."

Dag gave a short laugh. "In other words you think they may have. But," He added with narrowed eyes, "you don't intend moving us."

"Unless you wish to return to Kristiansund. I can't stop you. But I would much prefer it if you remained. We need to know more about them and what they've got planned."

"But, just keeping us under surveillance won't give you those answers, Rolf."

"True. I suspect what they really want to do is find out if you've still got the map, and what you may have gleaned from it. They wouldn't be interested in Finn, I shouldn't think, so he'd be safe."

"But I wouldn't be!"

"I can assure you we will make every effort to keep you safe." Rolf assured him.

"But you want me to be the spider and draw them into your web?"

"Who else? You will be invaluable. It may be the only chance we have of finding out what is behind this."

Dag shook his head and sighed. Rolf worried that he may have misjudged Dag. But he knew him well from their previous encounters and he was sure he wouldn't say no. However, back then he was a serving detective, now he was just an ordinary citizen and had no compulsion to help him.

Dag looked at Finn who was looking at him waiting to hear a response.

Gradually Finn broke into a smile. "You can't say no really, can you uncle Dag?"

Dag's doubts faded. If he had been alone, without Finn, he may well have said no and flown back to Kristiansund. Conversely, being with Finn he should definitely have said no. But, it was Finn and his smile that changed his heart. It was stupid, but it wasn't. Whatever these people had planned could be terrible, or maybe not; they didn't know. But if it was he could not ignore his duty. Not to the uniform this time, but to his country.

"Very well." Dag agreed. "What do we do?"

"Nothing. Just carry on being tourists. We'll do the rest. But I'll keep you informed at all times, of course. Randi may not be available for a few days, so I'll be your contact."

That concluded the agreement. Rolf rose, put his coat on and bade them goodbye.

"And wonder what Randi's doing?" Finn wondered aloud.

"Something undercover I imagine."

"And what about Ingrid. He didn't mention anything more her?"

"That's a point. I wonder what she's up to, and what Rolf's

doing about her? Although I think I – sorry we – have got enough to worry about without what she's up to."

"There's something I want to do tomorrow, Finn." Dag told Finn.

Finn looked at him uncertainly but waited for Dag to continue.

"Do you know who your mother's doctor was? I'd like to have a word with him."

"You still think there's a problem with mum's diagnosis?"

"I think she may have gone to the doctors too late for anything to be done. I want to find out if that's the case. Not that the doctor may tell me anything, what with patient confidentiality. But I can have ago."

Finn gave Dag the doctor's name and he'd got the phone number easily enough on his phone. He decided to male the call later from his hotel room when Finn was no with him.

10.

That evening they had a meal out again, just a burger from a well-known chain this night, not fancy French. Dag had kept an eye out for evidence of any minders but saw no-one, unless of course Rolf had got one employed as one of the hotel workers; but even then he had spotted no-one outside when they went to the burger joint. Dag even eschewed going for a beer to stay close to the hotel and not stray too far from it. Also, he was beginning to think that going for beers was not the best example to set for Finn, He didn't want to be blamed for encouraging him to take up a wayward life. Although if he eventually did join the police, he'd get enough practice then.

Dag bade Finn goodnight in the hotel corridor, saw that the had gone into his room and then went into his. The door card also set off the light inside the door. The bathroom was on his left and the short corridor meant that he couldn't see into all of his bedroom from that position, and would not have seen much anyway as the main bedroom light was not on. Even the street lights were blanked out by the curtains. The thought flashed through Dag's mind that he had left the curtains open, but he assumed that, when the room had been serviced, they had been closed. If he had thought a bit longer, he might have concluded that it would have been odd for a main to have closed the curtains in broad daylight.

He closed the door behind him and walked past the bathroom and into the main bedroom, turning and switching on the main light as he did so.

He stopped in his tracks.

He was not alone. Someone was sat on the end of his bed, lounging almost, looking at him, waiting for him.

She smiled.

Dag regained his composure. At least he hadn't shouted out in alarm, and she was, fortunately not pointing a weapon at him. She just sat and smiled.

Dag spoke first. "Ingrid." She looked as pretty and innocent as she did as the receptionist at the Flåm Hotel, all that time ago. But innocent she was not.

"Inspector Meldel." She said with the unchanged smile.

"I don't suppose it's much use me asking how you got in?"

"None at all. Are there any drinks in the mini-bar? I didn't want to be too presumptuous."

Dag opened it, took our two small cans of lager, and handed her one.

"It took a bit of doing." Ingrid told him. "Your friends are very good. But not good enough."

The two cans hissed as they were opened. Dag took a sip as did Ingrid.

"You've obviously come here for a reason." Dag began. "I'd be intrigued to know what it is."

"Coincidences." Ingrid told him. "I don't like them, and neither do you, so I'm told. The fact that you turned up in that restaurant and could have blown my cover was a little too much of one. I want to know what you're up to."

"Nothing to do with you, as it happens. And the young man with me was my nephew. He's been showing me around Oslo."

"You're taking holidays now?"

"Not exactly, no. I was attending my sister's funeral. What excuse do you have?"

"I work here. Well, I do now." Ingrid told him.

"Ah, yes, but what sort of work?"

Ingrid smiled. "That would be telling."

"I've told you, why shouldn't you tell me?"

"Your reason was not in the same sphere as mine. Anyway, you've given me your excuse for being here. But that can't be it, can it? Why would Rolf and his friends be taking such an interest in you? Why do they consider you important enough to have a round-the-cloak protection? I'm afraid your sister's funeral doesn't cover that."

"Whatever their reason, it had nothing to do with you."

"Ah, you said had, not has. There's a problem there with tense."

"Al right then, has." Dag corrected himself.

"Not good enough inspector."

Dag had no intention of telling her that he was no longer a D.I. That meant she did not know. And the more she did not know, the better.

"OK, I'll tell you. My friends thought you might have been involved in a near accident that myself and my nephew had. We now know differently."

Ingrid studied him, thinking, then said. "When was the accident?"

"Just after our dinner at your restaurant." he told her.

She thought again. "That timeline doesn't fit, does it. If you saw me at the restaurant there's no way I could have been involved in your accident. Why on earth would you immediately suspect me?"

"We thought you may have phoned someone right after you'd seen me."

"So it still leaves you with the coincidence of you eating at the restaurant where I was serving."

"Well, whether you like it or not, you must accept it was a coincidence."

"Like it or not I don't accept it."

"Very well. The investigation I'm involved with has nothing to do with you. Simple as that. You'll have to accept my word."

Ingrid drank some more of her lager. "OK. If its your word you're giving, I'll accept it. But it's messed up my plans."

Ingrid gave Dag a long hard look, then stood.

""I'm intrigued to know what all this is about. Sure you can't give me a little hint?"

Dag shook his head.

"Hmm. Then maybe you can help me."

"Me help you!" Dag laughed.

Ingrid shrugged. "Sometimes opposing lines cross over. I'm just wondering now whether this is one of them. Myself and my, how shall I say, colleagues, and they are not whom you might suspect, far from it, have a particular interest in certain current events. We wish to see them go in our preferred direction." She put a finger up to stop him speaking, as she could see that he was about to. "And that direction may be the same as your colleagues. Tell them about this meeting and what I've said. Maybe we can be of some use to each other."

"May I speak?" Dag asked. "If you think that Rolf and his employers would, for one moment, consider an alignment of sorts with you, I think you'll find that you're very much mistaken."

Ingrid smiled. "You have no idea who my colleagues – or should I say employers – are. Tell them. Tell them all I've said, We shall see who is right. Now, I should go. And, please, don't raise an alarm. Your nephew might find it unwise to stand in a lighted window. And you wouldn't want anything to happen to him would you?"

She slung her coat over her shoulder and brushed passed him, Dag let her go, waited a few seconds, rushed out, and knocked on Finn's door.

Finn opened it. Dag breathed a sigh of relief and calmed himself. He didn't actually think anything had happened, it was just a threat, and maybe one which had no substance to it. But you just never knew.

"Couldn't settle." Dag told him. "Wondered if you fancied a drink?"

In the foyer Dag looked at his phone. He typed in 'bar' and looked at the results. Not ten minutes away he saw the place he needed, a Whisky Bar.

"That's the place." He showed Finn. Finn raised an eyebrow. "It's OK, they serve beer as well, and they're open until late."

On the way Dag sent a text.

"Why are you suddenly going for a drink at this time of night? Not that I mind, it's just seems a bit weird, changing you mind like that."

"I had a visitor."Dag told him.

"A visitor? What, someone came to your room?"

"Someone was in my room."

"In your room?" Finn asked, puzzled.

"In my room when I got in. They were already there, they had let themselves in. And our protection didn't stop her."

"Her? Then, you said, 'her'." Finn pointed out. "Was it .."

Dag interrupted. "Yes, it was Ingrid."

"What the hell was *she* doing in your room? How did she get in? What did she want?" Finn asked all at once.

"How she got in, I don't know, not for sure. She was in my room to find out if I was looking for her, if I was involved with Rolf's people trying to find her. I tried to convinced her that it was purely a coincidence, and that I was here for a funeral and you were just my nephew."

"And did she believe you?"

"Of course not. But she told me that she was involved in 'certain current events', and that my colleagues – Rolf – might, in this case, be concerned about the same thing; that they may be able to work together, believe it or not."

They came to the bar and went inside. It wasn't too busy and they were able to buy a drink and find a table.

"What are you going to do?" Finn asked when they'd settled.

"I've already done it. I've sent a text to Randi or Rolf, whichever picks it up and told them we'd be here. No point wasting time. And I'd like to get us untangled from all of this as quickly as possible. It's dangerous."

"Dangerous?" Finn inquired.

"She made a threat and I take any threat from her seriously. So, it's better we extract ourselves from whatever all this is about. I don't want you getting involved any further, and I'm telling Randi or Rolf exactly that."

"What threat? What did she say?"

"Never mind precisely what. It's better you don't know. But I think we've done enough and got involved enough. It's time to say – well – enough is enough."

They both looked up as the door opened. After a brief survey of the people in the bar, Rolf came over to their table.

"Well-now Dag, what's all this about?" He asked.

Dag told him everything, all except the specific threat to Finn. He told Rolf that when he asked Finn to go to the bar and get some more drinks.

Rolf even managed a slight frown. "That she was able to enter your room so easily is worrying, and that she made such a threat. I hope it didn't have any substance, but we can't be too sure. I shall be having a word with your watchmen."

Finn arrived with the drinks. Even Rolf had a whisky.

"So," Rolf continued, "we shall have to find out what she's got such an interest in and how it, how did she say - intersects, with our interests. She hasn't given us much of a clue has she?"

"I'm sorry Rolf but I think we've done as much as we can. I don't myself, and especially Finn, getting involved any more deeply." Dag told Rolf.

Rolf took a sip of his whisky. "I see. That's unfortunate." He looked at Finn. What do you say Finn?"

"It's not up to him." Dag interrupted.

"Just wait a moment! I'm old enough to make up my own mind, uncle Dag. You're not my father you know. Thank god! But you can't make my mind up for my. I'm old enough to make my own decisions."

"You don't understand how dangerous it might be!" Dag implored.

"And did you understand everything when you joined the police?"

"This is different. It's way beyond normal police work." Dag told him.

"That hasn't stopped you in the past, why is it stopping you now?" Finn demanded to know.

"I'm no longer a policeman, that's why."

"In other words, you've had your life. I haven't lived mine

yet." Finn turned to Rolf. "I'm in if you want me to be."

Dag was, for a moment, lost for words. He didn't have a good answer because, of course Finn was right. He couldn't deny Finn his choices and chances in life, or interfere with them; he had no right to. But what was he going to do? If Finn made the decision to get involved he would have to be there to make sure he was as safe as could be. He had left all this behind, or so he thought. He took a gulp of whisky and let it burn through his throat and into his stomach.

"Well," Dag sighed, "I can't let you go into this alone, can I?"

Rolf had remained silent, listening to the family clash. "Well, that's all settled then. I imagine Ingrid will contact you. I wouldn't be surprised if she knows that we're having this meeting. I'll take a better look around when I leave, see if I can spot anyone. As soon as he gets in touch you will have to find out exactly where our interests intersect. It could be any number of things."

Rolf stood to put on his coat.

"I've just got one favour to ask." Dag said to him.

"And what would that be?" Asked Rolf.

"I - we - need some identification. I don't want to be blundering about without any. You should be able to provide that shouldn't you?"

Rolf paused, then nodded. "Very well, I'll get some to you by morning. Randi will bring them and update you if need be."

For the second time that night Dag said goodnight to Finn. He got into bed, but he could not sleep despite the whisky which should have helped. He got out of bed and sat on the end facing the mirror opposite him. On the table was a free notepad and a pen. He got up and sat at the desk in front of the mirror. He began to write notes on the paper. - just short ones. He tore them into pieces and, licking the paper, tried sticking them to the mirror's surface. They held. He sat back and studied them: the map, Ingrid, the woman at the station, the man she met (the Brigadier), the City Hall, and even Rolf and Randi as well as himself and Finn.

He was a detective again. He must put these things into some sort of order and work out what the links were, if indeed he could see any, which were not evident so far.

11.

Randi interrupted their breakfast.

"Here, these should help if you need any identification. They are time limited though." She told them, handing over a well-sealed brown envelope to each of them.

"Please?" Dag said offering her a seat.

"Thank you."

"Get a coffee for yourself, I'm sure they won't mind. Not that it's the best here."

"Water will be fine." Randi said pouring a glass for herself from a jug that was on the table.

"Thank you for these." Dag acknowledged. "Is there any more info?"

"Not unless you've been contacted by Ingrid. Although we are following up one or two leads in regards to her. The address she gave her employers was empty of course, and just as obviously she has not returned to work, much to their displeasure."

"Oh, OK. I think I've noticed an enhanced presence." Dag told her. He had noticed an additional waiter not usually on duty and there had been a cleaner at the end of the corridor much earlier than they would usually be about.

"I hope they weren't too obvious. But it doesn't matter too much really, does it? Their presence, if seen, is a preventative measure. If there is nothing else, I shall be getting along. You have our number, be sure to contact us immediately anything happens."

"Don't worry about that, I will." Dag assured her. "But I've got some personal things to see to today."

"I see." Randi said, but her eyes questioned him.

Dag gave way to her gaze. "It's about my sister's death. I want to get hold of more information, if I can."

Randi's eyes flicked to the ID in Dag's hand. "Those are only for official purposes, you know."

"Of course they are. You don't have to tell me." Dag replied, but noted that she didn't expressly forbid him using the ID's if necessary. At least, that would be his excuse.

When Randi had gone, Finn asked Dag what he was going to do about his mother's death.

"I'm going to call that doctor and see if he'll meet me. It's near you home isn't it?"

"Yes, quite close to the railway station."

"Do you want to come along with me? Maybe, you might need to go home?"

"What do I need to go home for?"

"Just thinking you might need to pick up some more belongings."

"I've got all I need. I don't want to go there. I don't want to meet *him*."

"I see. OK. But do you want to go to the doctors with me?"

Finn took a deep breath. "OK, I'll come. But I'm not sure why you need to do this. Why can't you just leave things as they are?"

"And if you were a detective, would you do that?"

Finn looked at his uncle. "No, I wouldn't. We've got to find out, haven't we, even if we might not like what we find. But it's the truth that matters isn't it?"

Dag nodded. "If we didn't try we might always be wondering - what if? It needs to be settled. I won't be able to easily rest if it isn't."

The doctor's surgery was a ten-minute walk from the station in the opposite direction to Finn's home. Dag was surprised that the doctor was willing to see him the same day. Dag had only given his name and said that he wanted to see him in relation to an investigation. He didn't say that he was or was not a policeman, but knew the tone to use, and the doctor didn't ask, he assumed.

Finn stayed outside. Dag went to the reception desk and introduced himself and then took a seat waiting to be called. The doctor came for him personally and took him to an examination room.

"We'll have to use this, I'm afraid." Doctor Halvorsen apologised.

Dag quickly flashed his new ID and took a seat that was offered.

"I've just a few questions. It's regarding one of your patients, or should I say someone who was one of your patients. I understand the privacy requirements, but the person has now passed away, so hopefully we can get around any directly medical questions. I'd like to concentrate more on interpersonal aspects of the case."

Doctor Halvorsen frowned. "I'm afraid I can't answer anything specific about a patient, you know that."

"As I said, this is someone who is dead, so no longer a patient per se. A family member is concerned that she may not have had a timely diagnosis." Dag held his hand up as he could see the doctor was about to protest. "No, not the fault of her doctor, but interference from elsewhere."

The doctor eased back into his chair and gave Dag a hard stare. "Who are you exactly? Can I see that ID again."

"Certainly you may." Dag took it out and showed him.

The doctors frown deepened. "What on earth has this got to do with a Government agency like yours?"

"There may be links to what could be called, by some, an extremist group. We are ring to establish what pressure they are putting on their members. This is highly confidential by the way, but I don't suppose I need to tell you that."

"Who exactly are you talking about? No, let me guess, it's Mrs Thomsen, isn't it?"

"You seem to have come to that conclusion pretty quickly. Can you tell me why?"

"Without going into medical details, I suppose so. She should have come to me much sooner. If she had, then at least we could have started treatment – or the hospital could. But it was left too late. I have to admit I wasn't happy with her explanation that she hadn't had any previous indications of the tumour, no headaches, no other symptoms. I just didn't believe it. It certainly seemed strange, but not entirely unusual."

"But you weren't satisfied. Why was that?"

"Her husband's attitude really. He turned up with her and hardly allowed her to speak; answering the questions for her. I had to keep asking him not to interrupt. He was a bit odd. Whatever I said he he was very offhand, as if he didn't believe me or refuted what I'd said. He was an unpleasant man."

"Could he have prevented his wife from obtaining treatment earlier?"

"If I was to guess, I'd say yes. But that's off the record."

"If you were concerned that a husband was slowly poisoning his wife you'd take action wouldn't you? Coercion is the same isn't it?"

"Not under the law, no. I have no legal responsibility for whether people decide to come for an examination or accept treatment. They are free to or not as they see fit. I can;'t force them."

"Just one more question, doctor. Do you know the group that Mr Thomsen belongs to?"

"I've heard of them, but I don't know anything about them, no."

"I see, thank you for your help. I think that's all I need to know. Unless I think of anything else at some stage, that should be it. And, once again, thanks for your help."

"So, it's their fault." Finn said when Dag had told him what had been said.

"Well, they're not allowing people to make sensible healthy

decisions are they. And if they're being coercive in other ways, they must be stopped in my opinion. There are too many of these sorts of groups around these days, some far worse perhaps than this one; I've bumped into them in the past."

"What are we going to do?"

"Let's put everything together properly, just as I would have done. Get all our facts right first before we make the next move. You should know quite a bit about them already, surely? Anything else we might be able to pick up from the internet, and then, a personal visit."

Finn smiled. "A real case." Then, his smile faded. "But they may have caused my mother's death."

"Well, they probably didn't cause it, but she might have lived longer if she'd had earlier treatment. They cut her life short. And to me, that's a crime. What do they call themselves?"

"The Church of Christ's Testament." Finn told him. "They're about a fifteen-minute drive down the road from Slependen; the train goes there."

"But in the other direction?" Dag guessed. Finn said that it was. "Well," Dag continued, "let's find out what we can about them before we give them a visit. It's time we got back to town and had some lunch."

They were on the train coming into the station when Dag's phone pinged.

'What news?'

It concerned Dag that Ingrid had managed to get hold of his phone number, he couldn't remember having given it to her, but the message must have been from her. Her phone number appeared but Dag knew only too well that she would have been using a throw-away phone for just this purpose.

'Can meet soon. Just at Central Station.' He replied.

He waited.

Ping! She had replied.

'Espresso House Citygate. Station. Five minutes.'

"Ingrid wants to meet." Dag told Finn. "A coffee shop at the far end of the station. She's very close."

"Coincidence?" Finn asked.

Dag smiled. "Doubt it. It's as if she knew we were on the train for her to be so close at the right time."

"How could she know that?"

"How do Rolf and Randi know where we are. I suspect they are tracking my mobile phone; yours as well perhaps. That, I'm OK with, but Ingrid being able to is a bit disconcerting. Anyway let's go and see what she has to say."

The main counter was open and facing the station shopping area and pedestrian thoroughfare. To the right was a seating area which went to the rear of the property.

Ingrid was already sat at the first table inside the open door and giving herself a good view of the thoroughfare. Dag and Finn

114

took seats facing her.

"Not drinking?" She asked Dag.

Dag looked at the counter. "Not my sort of coffee house."

Ingrid just gave a slight grin.

"So," she said, "what did your paymasters say?"

"They are not my paymasters. I don't require any pay for doing my duty to my country."

"I apologise. I too have a vision of what my duty is. But, you have met with Rolf, so what did he say?"

She even knew that he had met with Rolf straight after her visit. Rolf would be interested to know that, or concerned rather.

"You haven't given me much of a clue what you are on about. What interests do you think we have in common? It's no good presenting us with a blank piece of paper is it?"

"Two names: Jamba Caleb Rakha and Malidi Shomari Jata. I imagine you read the newspapers, if you haven't then that's what you should do. Tell Rolf that our interests converge with them. And there's someone else we are both interested in. Her name is Safia Mesay. She is here in Oslo. I'm sure they can trace her."

"I'm sure they can." Dag said.

"That is all for now. Tell him what I've told you. I have shown goodwill and would like him to do the same. I want something from him."

She paused so Dag had to ask. "And what is that?"

"When our collaboration is over I must be allowed to leave Norway free from arrest or detention."

"I see. Well, I'll put your put what you've said to him. Shall I text you or will you text me?"

"I'll text you and decide on where to meet and when." Ingrid told him. "For now," She added, rising, "I bid you farewell."

"All sounds a bit dubious to me." Finn said when she'd gone.

"Hmm. I think she meant what she said. Fancy something to eat? I'm hungry."

"Here?" Finn suggested.

"No let's find somewhere else. I'll text Randi when where settled elsewhere."

"Are you trying to protect Ingrid somehow?"

"I think for now it's best to keep the two sides apart. Best for them and best for us. Let's go back to my favourite cafe. At least I can get some decent coffee."

Randi joined them within ten minutes of Dag texting her.

She nodded. "It was one of the things we thought she may have been alluding to. Now we can direct our attentions to in that direction and onto those people. What have you read in the papers?"

Dag grimaced. "Not a lot, I'm afraid."

"Jamba Caleb Rakha is the President of Ikebaje." Finn provided the information for Dag. "He's about to get the Nobel Peace Prize – well, next month. The other guy's the Brigadier that the woman who dropped the map met at the airport. He's the President's brother-in-law; the one who has just become a defence attaché at their embassy."

"Thank you, Finn." Randi said. "Perhaps you could update your uncle on the details."

"And it all has a link to that map." Said Dag darkly. "Now, that really is a coincidence."

"Is it?" Randi asked.

"I can't see how it could be otherwise. But there again, as I always say, I don't like coincidences, but this one just seems too far-fetched."

"Hmm, well, have a think about it. I'd like to know if it really was or wasn't. Meanwhile, I'll talk to Rolf, and I'm sure he'll be agreeable to some cooperation between Ingrid and her people and us. I'll text you."

"Who exactly are 'her people'? Dag asked.

"An interesting question and one I can't give you an answer at this time." Randi told him.

"I see. Fair enough. I'll await your call and then I'm sure Ingrid will get back to me. She seems to have as good an idea of where I am as you are."

"Does she now? How interesting. Let's keep it that way for now."

Having filled themselves as best they could with vegetarian wraps and hot coffee Dag and Finn strolled back to the hotel.

At his bedroom door Dag told Finn he'd update himself on every the web had to offer on the President and his brother-in-law and asked Finn if he could search out anything more on The Church of Christ's Testament.

They could discuss what each had found out over a drink and a meal in the evening.

Finn fancied a Thai meal, so they found one not too far away.

"I wish I'd taken a bit more interest in the news over the past few days." Dag told Finn. "If I had I may have made some connections earlier. It's very thoughtless of me. The President and the Peace Prize are linked to Oslo, of course, the Brigadier, his brother-in-law is linked to him, the brigadier is linked to that woman, and that woman is linked to the map. And I'm linked to the map. The links are all there. But what is behind them? The map suggests a possible attack or interference in the Nobel prize-giving, but as you said it's not being held there this year. It's at the University. That's the conundrum. That's where the link breaks. And what's behind the link between the Brigadier and Safia Mesay? It may not be unfriendly, it may be benign - it could even be personal. The perplexing thing are the marks on that map. What do they mean?"

Dag had been thinking and talking aloud the very things he had put together in front of his mirror and pieces of paper earlier.

They both lapsed into silence continuing to eat their different Pad Thai dishes.

"You forgot Ingrid in your chain of links." Finn said after a mouthful.

"And E15. I've left them outside the direct chain for now. They're just trying to fathom the same things we are. Although I'd bet they've got more info than us. What about the Church?"

"Not a lot. It was started by the Pastor, as he calls himself, Jorgen Lageson. But I can't find anything on the web about him having a proper qualification, and it's the only one around as far as I can tell. He started it up himself. He must have had some money though. The land and building of the church was all paid for."

"Sounds like he either really believes he has something new to offer people and wasn't able or willing to get proper training and accreditation with an established church, or his ideas wouldn't have been accepted by them. Either that or he has simply found a way of living of the proceeds of others instilling a belief in him. A cult if ever I've heard of one. I think we'll have a chat with Pastor Jorgen Lageson."

"In the morning?" Finn asked.

"Yes, tomorrow morning."

12.

"I'll stay around the corner." Finn told Dag outside the church. "I don't think it'll help with me there. He doesn't like me."

"Fair enough. It will probably be best I faced him alone."

The church was a quite new building on the edge of a small industrial estate. The walls were wood but, unusually, black, and all the windows were were just below roof level. The sign on the fascia above announced 'The Church of Christ's Testament'. A main door led into the church but there was a side door that had a sign for the office. On a corner further along the fascia were two security cameras; one pointing at the main door, the other at the office door. Dag pressed the integral door bell and speaker on the office door. There was a click and a man's voice told him to come in and a further click of the door unlocking.

'A lot of security for a church.' Dag thought.

He turned the door handle and went in.

There was a long corridor, the length of the building, and at the end an open office door. A figure moved into the light from the door. Dag could only see who it was in silhouette.

"Please, come in." Came the man's voice.

Dag walked forwards. "Mr Lageson?"

"Yes." Lageson said as they shook hands.

"Dag Meldel." Dag told him.

They had entered the room and Dag could now see the man more clearly. He was tall and slim, thin one might say, with dark hair and sharp features, wearing fine metal-rimmed glasses. He offered Dag a chair one side of the desk; he took the opposite.

"To what do I owe the pleasure?" Lageson asked as they sat.

"It's about one of your parishioners." Dag said.

"I prefer the word 'believer'." Lageson countered. "We have no parish and do not believe in the hierarchy of such constructs."

"I see, well, one of your believers then. Her name is or rather was, Kristine Thomsen."

Dag saw a slight flicker of the eyelids when he mentioned his sister's name.

"Ah, yes, one of our dear departed. She has been called by God to join him in eternal paradise. Her suffering is now over ,and she is joyful in heaven."

"Yes, her suffering. You are correct that it's now over. But I'm not so sure that she was joyful in the, possibly, unnecessary length time that she suffered. She could have been treated at a far earlier stage, could she not?"

Dag could see the pastor's face tighten.

"We place ourselves in the hands of God, Mr Meldel, He decides how our lives are lived and how they end. It is not for us to interfere with the workings of God."

"But she could have been treated. Surely you cannot deny people treatment for diseases and medical conditions?"

"Our faith in God treats not only our soul but our physical being as well. I grant that natural remedies may be used, after all they have been placed upon this earth by Our Lord himself and there can be no reason why they cannot be used. But we do not agree that man should interfere with the natural order. But let me ask you Mr Meldel, who are you anyway, and why these questions?"

"Kristine was my sister." Dag told him.

"Ah," Lageson said, leaning further back in his chair, "you are the ex policeman Anders has told me about. He thought you may come asking questions. And I have one for you; where is Finn? You have taken him from his home and his family."

"Finn is old enough to make his own decisions and I haven't

pressured him into anything he didn't want to do, Mr Lageson. And as far as you saying I'm an ex policeman, that is correct, but I'm currently working for the Government which Anders did not know. Here, my credentials." Dag showed him his ID.

Lageson frowned. "Why would such a Government agency have any interest in this? We are a peaceful organisation."

"The Government likes to take an interest in many organisations such as yours. Some might say a cult." Dag told him. "If it were an Islamic one you'd hardly be surprised at all, I suspect."

"How dare you. We are the true religion. We are not a cult, we are a registered organisation. Our founding principle is one of peace. But that may be difficult for people like you to understand. Your sort, your Governments, they all talk of peace, but we know that behind it are lies. They talk peace on one hand and support infamous regimes on the other, they support beliefs that have nothing to do with the true religion, that promote murder and mayhem. What peace does that give us? We have seen time and again that it only brings violence. They hand out awards and prizes for peace to idolaters and murderers, and expect us to praise them. We do not, we condemn them, and God will extract his justice."

Dag was taken aback. "An interesting tirade Mr Lageson, but it does not address the matter of my sister, and if I find that there has been any direct cause for her death because of your preachings, be assured, I will not let it rest. Thank you for seeing me. I think that will be all for now."

Dag stood and, amid silence from Lageson, opened the door and let himself out.

"What happened?" Finn asked.

"Well, it's just about as near to a religious cult as I can imagine. But, I suppose, other people might disagree. As far as your mother's concerned, I'm pretty sure it was pressure from him that meant she didn't see a doctor earlier. Not that there was anything you could take as evidence in a court of law., and it would mean that your father would be the obvious one to press any charges if they could be pressed, and I don't think that's likely, do you?"

Finn looked a little crestfallen. "No, he wouldn't. What about me? Could I take Jorgen Lageson to court?"

"It would be the flimsiest of cases I'm afraid. Do you have any direct evidence yourself that could be used in court? Any documentary evidence? Even if you said you heard conversations to support your case it would need corroboration, otherwise it would only be hearsay. Would your sister or father confirm any such conversations? I doubt it."

"So, there's nothing we can do?"

"Well, there's still the doctor. The problem there is that he can't force any patient to have procedures or medicines against their will, and again, there's no evidence that your mother refused treatment against her will. But, I suppose we can see if we can put some more pressure on him. I wonder if he's had any other problems with members of that church? Maybe, he has. If so, we might be able to get him on side. I'll see if I can meet him again."

"Oh well, that's something I suppose."

"Tell me." Dag asked Finn. "How much contact did you have with the church? Were you made to attend any of the services?"

"I went along a few times, but to be honest, it was all a bit over the top. All that stuff about God being able to heal everyone who was a true believer. I suppose that's something against him isn't it?"

"Unfortunately people have the right to say such rubbish. Anything else?" Dag asked. He had an uneasy feeling about things that Jorgenson had said.

"All sorts of stuff. It didn't matter where we lived, where we were, there was no parish, the world was the parish – or *his* parish. I suppose he thinks that his church is the only church. And then there was all his preaching about Governments, Christian ones that is, and how they had strayed from the path."

"Did he ever mention what he'd do about that?"

Finn shook his head. "Not that I remember. He just blamed the Government when things happened. Like that Islamist extremist last year. He was pretty angry about that, saying all sorts of things."

"Anything like reprisals or retaliation?"

Finn was thoughtful. "Vengeance will be ours, I think he said, and something about God's retribution."

"And did you take that as being God's avenging or someone more mortal?"

"I didn't think he meant doing anything himself, if that's

126

what you mean."

"But what about inciting others?"

Finn gave him an uncertain look. "I didn't take it that way. And , after all, that was a couple of years ago, and I haven't been there for what, more than a year."

"Hmm, well, a lot can change in a couple of years."

"Why are you asking me about all that anyway? I thought we'd gone because of my mother."

"There were things he said that have got me thinking." Dag admitted. "Things that worried me. Things that I think Rolf and his people may be interested in. It may be nothing, but it's best to be sure."

"You think he might do something bad? Against some Muslims perhaps? I don't think anyone in the congregation would be involved in anything like that. They're a bit weird and, yes, they've been taken in by him, but I can't see any of them doing anything stupid."

"I expect you're right." Dag assured him. "But I'd like to be on the safe side. I'll ask Rolf or Randi if they can look into him. And maybe there's something in his past that we can get on him, if we can't stop him peddling his nonsense any other way."

The train was once more pulling into the Central Station when Dag got a text.

"Ingrid wants to meet us at the Hard Rock Café, near to the University Building. Is it far from here?" Dag asked Finn.

"A straight fifteen-minute walk along Karl Johans Gate."

Dag looked at his watch. It was 13:45. "She says at 15:00. We've got an hour spare."

"I'm hungry." Finn hinted.

"Very well let's get something to eat first, I could do with a decent coffee myself."

"Usual place." Finn asked.

"Is it on the way?"

"Not far out of the way."

After their stop for food, they only just the Hard Rock Café in time. It was busy and the place was large.

"Can you spot her?" Finn queried.

"Not immediately. Not to worry we'll take a seat, I'm sure she'll find us."

Ingrid appeared as if out of nowhere from behind them when they were seated.

"So, what do you want us for?" Dag asked.

"A little job you may be able to help me with. I'm not sure if your compatriots are dealing with it, although I suspect they are. However, I'd like another eye on it, another viewpoint, so to speak. It concerns Ms Safia Mesay. I'm afraid I may have compromised myself with her and can't continue with my surveillance."

"She's sussed you." Finn smiled.

"Possibly. But it's safer to be sure rather than sorry."

"If Rolf is also dealing with her, why us? We're not experts in surveillance. We'd stand out like a sore thumb."

"I disagree. You can be so obvious, you can be unnoticeable. Unless, of course she recognises you as the man she bumped into at the station; then, she might begin to wonder. Otherwise, acting as conspicuous tourists I think she will discount you as a threat."

"A threat? And what would it mean if she thought we were one?"

"If there was any indication of that, I'm sure you would be wise enough to back off as quickly as possible."

"And what about Rolf? We'd be stepping on his toes. He'd not be happy about it."

"Tell him. I think you'll be surprised at his answer."

"That sounds like I've already been stitched up by both of you." Dag complained.

"I've not made any specific arrangement, but I've heard they may have had the same problem as myself. So, I'm sure he would welcome your involvement."

"Ha!" smiled Finn again. "You've both messed up. That's a

good one that is."

"I'm sure," said Dag, "you are going to give me some information about Ms Mesay, otherwise we wouldn't know where to start."

Ingrid passed him an envelope. "All you need to know is there. You can use that mobile number to pass any info to me. What you tell Rolf is your own affair, I promised we would share anything of use."

She rose, bid them good afternoon, and left.

"You could have said no." Said Finn.

"I could. But I don't think it would have made much difference. Rolf would be the next one in line to pressure us by the sound of it. And don't forget, I want a favour from him; information about pastor Lageson. It's a trade off."

"That's true. So, what's in the envelope?"

Dag opened it and read it.

"Some addresses. One is the Nagamba consulate; they haven't got a full Embassy I suppose, there's one at Skillebekk in Oslo where Safia Mesay is living. Another is a hotel, it seems our Brigadier Malidi Shomari Jata is staying here in some style; the Grand Hotel."

"That's just down the road from here, back towards the station, almost right opposite the Parliament building. We passed it on the way here." Finn told him.

"Hmm, fancy a drink in a hotel bar?" Dag asked. It was now gone four in the afternoon and seemed late enough in the day to order beers.

"Aren't you going to try and find Safia Mesay first? That's who Ingrid wanted us to keep an eye on." Finn asked him.

"We have her address, she can wait. Let's start close to hand. I'm not going to be dictated to by Ingrid. In fact, I think it's better we work on this ourselves, in our own way, rather than be working directly for her; or Rolf for that matter." Dag told him.

The hotel entrance was as five star as one could imagine. Dag strode straight to the reception counter which was currently free of any customers and held his new ID in front of the receptionist. She frowned and asked him how she could help.

"My reason for being here is highly confidential, as you can image, so, please, not a word to anyone. Is that clear?"

"Yes, of course." The receptionist looked both suitably impressed and disconcerted.

Dag made a point of looking around to make sure no-one was about other than Finn who stood a few steps behind him.

"You have a Brigadier Jata staying here. I just need to know if he is in his room." Dag asked.

The receptionist asked him to wait a moment, and she went and checked the keys.

"No, the Brigadier does not appear to be in his room." She told him.

"Thank you. Please do not alert him to the fact that we have asked about him. Meanwhile," he said, looking over to his left where there was seating in what appeared to be part of the bar, "is that the bar?"

She told him it was. He thanked her, nodded to Finn, and they went to take a seat where they could keep an eye on the reception area.

"What good is this going to do?" Finn asked when they'd got their drinks.

"I want to see him, in person, that's all; get a feel for him. He's involved with this Mesay woman somehow, and I'd like to watch not just her, but him as well. You can learn a lot about people just by watching them for a while. Ingrid may want us to watch Mesay, but that doesn't give us a complete answer to what's going on, does it? If we're going to get involved in this, we'll have to know about both of them, and anyone else who comes to our attention along the way. If we're going to do it, let's do it properly."

"Right!" Finn said emphatically.

They were on a second small beer and the time had ticked on to past five when the Brigadier appeared. It wouldn't take a moment for anyone to realise it was him. He was tall, well over six feet, broad and muscular, and walked, or one might say marched and strutted like a peacock, into reception. He at least wore an expensive suit rather than a military uniform.

He did not have to wait for his key. It was ready for him, and was handed to who must have been a junior officer, his aide. He did not deign to take the key himself.

As he walked to the lifts, he glanced over at where Dag and Finn were watching him. His look made Finn wince. There was a fierce coldness in his eyes, which narrowed as he looked at first Finn and then Dag. There was a scar on each of his cheeks which Dag wondered if they were inflicted in some sort of fight or, as some country's customs dictate, the result of a form of tribal ritual or custom.

The Brigadier turned swiftly away and disappeared towards the lifts. But the other officer had briefly stopped behind him and also looked at them. He was slimmer, thin almost, and a good few inches shorter. But he too had the marks on his cheeks.

"Well, now." Said Dag. "He's interesting."

"Interesting? Scary I'd say. Don't think I'd trust him."

"I wonder how he compares to his brother-in-law, the President?"

"Hang on." Finn said, taking his phone and finding a picture of him.

A very different face looked out at them from the phone. Neither fat nor thin but the look of him, with much kinder seeming eyes; a;though he was smiling rather than glaring like the Brigadier. But the one that that was noticeable was that he had no markings on his cheeks.

"Interesting." Dag concluded aloud. "If those marks are a

tribal thing, then our President doesn't look like he's from the same tribe as the Brigadier."

"There's quite a mix of tribes and different religions in the country." Finn told him. "You wouldn't think it was big enough for that amount of diversity, it's only a very small country."

"The place Ms Mesay comes from, Nagamba, is that right next door. I'm not exactly a Geography expert."

"About half of each country borders the other, and they are about as mixed."

"Not exactly a recipe for peaceful co-existence."

"That's why there's always been some sort of fighting or war going on. Until lately of course, which is why the President's been given the Peace Prize."

"But it's not so peaceful now is it? There's fighting going on again."

"Yes, it all started with the murder of some villagers, well, quite a few, up to a hundred it's said. Both countries are blaming each other. Each blaming the other's army, and each army blaming rebels and insurgents claiming it's not them."

""Yes, I read about it. I've got a feel for what's going on here and I don't like it."

"So have I, and I don't either." Finn told him nervously.

Dag looked at his watch. "Well, how about checking out Ms Mesay's address?"

"And something to eat?" Finn asked hopefully.

"You're always hungry." Dag moaned.

"It's the beer, it makes me hungry." Finn told him.

The stood to leave. Dag put his arm out to stop Finn, then told him to sit.

A woman had just walked into reception.

"I don't think we need to go to her address, she's just come to us." Dag told him.

Dag had recognised the coat. It was the same one she'd been wearing that day at the station. They watched and waited. Safia Mesay didn't take long at reception before she too went to the lifts. Dag got up and peered around the corner to see which floor the lift stopped at. The light showed it on the third floor before beginning to return. He waited until the desk was clear of some people checking in and then questioned the receptionist. The answer was obvious, but Dag liked to make sure. She had gone to the Brigadier's room.

"Another drink I think." Said Dag when he returned. "But coffee this time. Food will have to come later. For now we wait until she leaves. Then, we follow her."

They waited, and waited. An hour passed.

Dag looked worried. "I wonder?" He said aloud.

"Wonder what?" Asked Finn.

"I wonder if she spotted us or whether she was warned that

we were down here. In which case she may have left by another means."

"Like a fire escape?"

"That or stairs. There must be stairs as well as lifts."

The receptionist confirmed there were.

Dag looked at the time. It was now quarter past six.

"I'm sure she can't still be with the Brigadier. Let's check out her address. You never know she might turn up there. We can at least check the area out and see if she's at home."

"What are you going to do, knock on her door and say hello?"

"No." Dag grimaced, not liking the sarcasm. "It's dark isn't it. Her apartment's lights will be on if she's at home. Let's splash out and get a taxi. I'll put it on expenses for Rolf."

However, they had only got to stand outside the hotel ready to flag one down when Dag's phone pinged again. This time it was Rolf.

"Oh, well." Dag said. "No time for her apartment, Rolf wants to see us. He's not far away."

"The usual cafe?"

"Yes."

"You've been stirring things up a bit." Rolf told them. "Brigadier Jata has made a complaint that he was being spied on by two men; one older, one younger. Naturally it was denied. The Foreign Office dealt with it, so it was easy to do so. We come under the Defence Ministry and were not asked. But he's got you in his sights. By the by, what were you doing at his hotel anyway? I thought it was Ms Mesay you were supposed to be tailing?"

"It was, and we were." Dag explained. "It was lucky we were there. Ms Mesay was visiting the Brigadier, but unfortunately avoided us when she left. She must have used a different exit."

"Yes, one of our men saw her go in." Rolf admitted.

"We were just on our way to check out her address." Dag told him.

"Well, you can save yourself some time. She's not at home at the moment."

Dag sighed. "I really don't know why we're doing this. Surely you and Ingrid are both keeping tabs on her? Why ask us to do the same?"

"It was not us that asked. It was Ingrid, and I'm not sure why. But if we're going to find out why, then we need you to carry on."

"Basically we are just being used." Dag grumbled.

"To find out what Ingrid's about, I'm afraid the answer is yes. Why she is using you, I haven't a clue. That's what I need to know."

137

"Well, if there's no point checking out her apartment, I think we'll call it a night. And we'd better be careful to keep away from the Brigadier in future."

"No, no. Please keep tabs on him as well. It'll be good to see if he gets jittery. We'll have a man close by anyway, so you should be fine."

"Really?" Dag said very dubiously. Then said. "I've a favour to ask you before you go."

Dag explained that he wanted to know more about the pastor, Jorgen Lageson, and asked Rolf for anything he had on the man.

"Interesting." Rolf mused. "The name rings a bell, but I can't quite put my finger on it. I'll find out what I can and get back to you. For now, I'll bid you good night."

"Enough is enough for today." Dag told Finn. "Let's get something to eat, you must be starving by now." He smiled.

13.

Dag and Finn had just finished breakfast and were about to go to Dag's room to stick the 'fact' papers on the mirror and think things over again when Ingrid sent a text.

"Safia is at home. That's all it says." Dag relayed it to Finn.

"So, we go there?" Asked Finn.

"Hmm, yes. A bit odd though. It's as though she knew that we'd known that she wasn't there last night, that we should be told that Safia was there now."

"Like she knew everything that happened last night?"

"Yes, like that." Dag frowned.

"Ingrid seems to know an awful lot about our movements."

"Yes, and I don't like it."

"You don't think ...." Finn didn't finish the sentence.

Dag finished it for him. "That Rolf and her are in it together?"

"It's a bit of a coincidence, and I've learnt how you don't like *them*."

"Well, let's play along. But we must be careful, we mustn't taker any risks. It's all beginning to get a bit unnerving."

Finn looked at his phone. "There's a tram every ten minutes. It'll take us straight there. Number 13. We can catch it on Fred Olsens Gate."

"OK Let's go."

The Skillebekk area was a conglomeration of apartment blocks each about five stories high set out more or less in a grid; all reasonably new. The gardens were well-tended and Dag didn't think an apartment would have been particularly cheap to but or to rent. Safia Mesay's apartment was in a block to the North of the area just one street in from the main road.

They walked from the tram stop, Dag taking notice of the area and its buildings. Just before the tram has stopped Dag noticed a large white semi-classical building which had, above its door, letters that read, 'The Norwegian Nobel Institute.' He wondered if this again was merely coincidence; that Safia was living so close to the offices of the organisation which was giving the Peace Prize to the Brigadier's brother-in-law, the President. From the main road they turned into the housing estate, then right again into the road where Safia's apartment was.

They knew the apartment's number but had no idea where about in the building it was. But next to it was a semi underground parking area which would be useful. Above it was a wide garden area which several of the blocks overlooked. Hanging around there would have them noticed in no time. The entrance to Safia's block was at the rear of that. There were two doors, depending in which part of the building one lived. By each door were bell pushes, with the numbers of the apartments handily written on them. Safia's number, 501, was at the first door.

"She's on the top floor." Dag told Finn who was peering over his shoulder.

"There's a sort of roof terrace up there." Finn said.

"Hmm, she'll have a good view across the open space and much of the road. Any sort of OP's going to be difficult. She's the one that's got the area covered. It's only at the back, here, where we can cover the comings and goings. And the only way we'll do that is by getting a car. It can park along this dead end, like the others."

Several cars were already parked along it in parking bays, but there were free spaces.

"You'll have to hire one." said Finn.

"Another one for the expenses." Answered Dag. "Let's not hang around."

They had just moved off and were about to turn the corner in the main street when they heard the door opening. Dag had just passed beyond it but Finn managed to glance round.

He quickly moved forward. "It's her." He hissed.

They both ran to the parking area, dived into the undercover part and hid behind two parked cars. Safia walked passed. They heard her footsteps move away and came out from under cover. She had just gone around the corner taking the street to the main road. They followed. Hanging back they let her get well ahead of them. Dag told Finn to go ahead so that they were now appear to be together and he followed.

When Safia reached the main road she turned right. Both Fin and Dag hurried forward so that they could both look around the corner and keep her in view. She continued up the road. Dag and Finn changed places with Dag leading, still keeping a good distance between himself and Safia. Dag had told Finn that regularly changing the lead would make them less apparent.

Safia came to the tram stop. Behind them Dag and Finn could hear the sound of a tram. It passed them. Dag new they wouldn't be able to get to the tram stop in time to catch it and wasn't sure that it was a good idea anyway. She might well recognise them from the night before.

"She's on the number 12." Finn said.

"Where does that go?"

"Much the same route as the 13. Goes past the Parliament then on towards the Station, on the other side of the square outside our hotel."

"The Parliament isn't far from her country's consulate." Dag said, taking the paper with the addresses out of his pocket. Akersgate. Let's check it out. When's the next tram?"

"About eight minutes."

They didn't hang around when they walked down the Southern end of Akersgate. Besides the shops, a quick look at the plaques on the walls next to the building's entrances showed a variety of company offices; lawyers, accountants, importer and exporters, and those without any indication what they might get up to. But several were embassies or consulate offices; Ikebaje and Nagamba being two of them, and only a few doors apart. Dag was also sure that at least one car, if not two, parked along the road, might be security of one sort or another.

It was interesting that the two countries had offices so close together. Dag pointed out that as they were so close, both here and as neighbouring countries, was it necessary for Safia Mesay to visit the Brigadier at the hotel when she could have easily seen him in their embassy. He was sure that it pointed to their meeting being one that they did not wish others in their corresponding offices to know about. They were up to something.

Dag needed a coffee. His favourite cafe was only a five-minute walk away along a straight road when they turned left out of Akersgate. It was not only the coffee Dag liked about the place, it was the fact that it had two walls of complete glass that gave a view of everything going on outside; along all four streets of the crossroads at the corner where it stood.

Sat where they could get the best view, Dag received an email.

"From Rolf. He's got my personal email address now. It just says 'info for you', and there's a file attached." He told Finn.

There was silence between the two of them whilst he opened and read it.

"Some facts about our pastor, Jorgen Lageson. He's had quite a chequered career."

"What does it say?" Finn asked, as Dag became quiet re-reading it.

"He was quite an activist when he was younger at University here in Oslo. He studied Political Philosophy. A left-winger then, significantly to the left so it says. He was a member of the NKP Communists, but became disillusioned with the way the party supported the Soviet union. Later he swapped over to supporting the Fatherland Party when it was set up in 1990."

"Quite a change that, isn't it?" said Finn.

"Yes, about as right wing as you would get at the time, but it dissolved in 2008. Then, he went over to the New Future Coalition after he left University. Not that that lasted long, it got merged with the Christian Unity Party. He certainly tries all sorts of political parties, but seems like he couldn't find as home in any of them. Then, he went back to University. Started a course in Theology and Religion but didn't see it through.

Now, there's a page on his police record. A couple of minor offences – speeding and such, but, hmm, this is interesting; Two accusations of assault. Not fights, sexual. Both cases were dropped when the victims withdrew their claims. Have you heard about his at all, Finn? It's not something that's easy to keep quiet."

Finn shook his head. He looked a bit pale. But he said nothing.

Dag looked back at the email. "Ah, I'm not surprised. He wasn't in Oslo then, he was in Stavanger. That's where it looks like he set up his first church, or chapel; it was a pretty small affair." Dag paused, thinking. "He couldn't have made much money from it, unless his followers were very generous. I wonder how he got the money to build the church he's got now?" He didn't wait for an answer. "He moved to Oslo from Stavanger five years ago. Rolf's made a note at the end; Lageson, it is believed, has kept in touch with some ex members of the Fatherland Party and whom he may have got his funds for building the church. But, no-one has ever thought it necessary to make any investigations. His accounts appear to be in order."

"A pretty confusing picture of the man, which makes him a pretty confusing person. I wouldn't have thought him all that religious looking at his past. Maybe it gives him the feeling of power he never achieved through politics." Dag concluded. "Are you OK?" He asked, looking at Finn who seemed miles away.

"Sorry, yes. I was listening. It was a lot to take in that's all."

"Are you worried about your sister? I mean, that bit about sexual assaults. Are you sure you've not heard anything?"

"No, no, I haven't heard anything." Finn assured Dag.

But Dag was not so sure. He had seen that look and attitude before. Finn was hiding something, Dag knew it. But he also knew that, in such circumstances, it was better not to push to hard to find out what it was. He must bide his time and try and get it out of the young man slowly and gently. What worried him most was that it wasn't Anette who was in danger, but that it may have been Finn himself who had been threatened or exposed to an assault in the past.

Dag decided to change the subject. "We should make plans on keeping Safia under surveillance. As you said, we'll need a car, I'll have to hire one. Can you look on your phone?"

"There's three at the railway station. One of them is just around the side of the hotel." Finn told him.

"Well, let's go and get one."

14.

Dag and Finn had had managed to find a space to park the car in the side road not too far from the door to Safia's apartment block, but far enough, hopefully, not to be noticed. At least the nights were drawing in and darkness had fallen by 15:45 which gave them cover. Also, two large trees, now without leaves, also gave them partial cover from its branches from being spotted from a window, although that also lessened their view as well.

'Why oh why,' thought Dag, 'are we doing this and not Rolf's people? And why did Ingrid need us to do it as well?' There was certainly very odd about it, but until Dag could put his finger on exactly what it was, he had to play along. The main thing was to be careful, not to get themselves into any situation that put them in danger rather than the people they were now working for. And what did they want to know about Safia's movements? What could he tell them that they couldn't find out for themselves? It was, he repeated to himself, a bit of a conundrum, and one he had to get to the bottom of. But how?

Maybe Safia would be the answer. And the only way to get it from her was to do what they were doing, keeping an eye on her.

"How good is your phone at taking pictures?" Dag asked.

"About as good as any. I can always enhance them afterwards' easy enough with the software that's around."

"Good. Take a shot of anyone going in or out."

Dag looked at his watch. "How about you take the first shift. I'll have a nap and take over later until she leaves in the morning; if she does."

Dag pulled his coat around him. It was going to be a long and cold night. The cloud was getting heavier and there was the threat of rain in the air. At least the hotel had given them a flask of coffee. Even if it wasn't the best, it was hot.

Finn zipped up his ski jacket and also settled down, keeping his eyes on the apartment door.

Some people came and went, mostly came, and who must have been the other occupants. Finn took a photo of them each time. It was 21:25 – he had made a note of checking his watch each time he took a photo – that someone came to the door and rang one of the bells. It was not a resident. Finn got his camera and zoomed in to take a picture. His finger touched the button and the phone made its pretend shutter click.

Hardly before it was taken, his heart beat faster. He froze, looking at the person on the screen. He took another shot. The caller said something, the door opened, and then they went in.

Finn had recognised who it was. He sat, bemused, letting it sink in. He should have shaken Dag then, woken him and told him, but he remained staring at the now closed door.

What was going on? What connection would mean that Safia would have them as a visitor? That is, if the person was visiting Safia. They might not be; probably wasn't. They were visiting someone else, another resident entirely, and it was just a coincidence. But Finn had heard Dag talking about his distrust of coincidences and knew that he rarely believed anything was one. But in this case it had to be. Finn decided that, for now, he would keep it to himself. He had gone through the arguments in his mind but there was more to it than that; he could not reveal the visitor for another reason.

He waited. The person had to leave before Dag woke and took over. It was only about three quarters of an hour later that they left. Finn didn't bother taking a picture this time. He knew who it was. He simply watched them go. Finn kept wondering; was it Safia they were seeing? It must surely be someone else. But what was the likelihood? What was the chance that that person had come to this very apartment block at the very moment to see someone else? Very little was the answer. The answer that Finn did not want to come to. He must ask the question of them himself.

Dag woke at 01:00. He asked Finn if anything of interest had happened and Finn told him it hadn't. Finn showed Dag how to use the camera on his phone, but not before he had saved a copy of the one picture in a file on Dropbox. They swapped places so Dag had a better view, had a cup of coffee, and then settled

149

down for the rest of the night.

Finn had a restless night and slept little. As morning came people began to leave for work. They watched and waited. It was 09:48 before Safia left the block. Dag took his time before setting off to follow her. He wanted to keep a distance. Once again she went up to the main road, stood at the tram stop, and waited for the tram. Dag had to park in a lay-by outside an office block whilst she waited. She boarded the tram. They followed. She alighted at a stop near Akersgate and then walked to her consulate.

"She doesn't start work early, does she?" Dag muttered.

"What next?" Finn asked him.

"First I get a shower, then a late breakfast. I need to get something to eat before I take some pills. You probably need the same. There's a station car park, a bit expensive, but I'll bill Rolf."

"And then?"

"It's probably best we take it in turns to keep an eye on the consulate, clock her when she comes out. It would be difficult not to be obvious in that street, but I'm not going to worry about that. I'd already made my mind up that what we need to do, have to do, or shall I say are expected to do, is to be more obvious."

"Why's that? Why let them know we're watching them?"

"Because then they will make some sort of move. Hopefully not against us. But I think that's exactly what Ingrid wanted. I'm not sure why, and why she couldn't do it herself, as you know, and neither does Rolf. But I'm sure both of them are using us, rather than their own people, specifically to see what they do."

"So, as you said, they're just using us; we're just pawns."

"Pawns maybe, but pawns who realise what they are, and that way we can take precautions."

Finn frowned. "What about that car which nearly killed us? Nothing's been done about it. Everyone told us that it must have been Safia or the Brigadier behind it because she knew who we were. But that can't be possible. If it was, surely they would have acted again?"

"They might have tried once and then be put off trying again now that the police and Rolf's people got involved. But your right. There's something odd about it. How could they have known who we were, how could they have found us so easily. It just doesn't gel. There's more to that car attack than meets the eye, but I'm at a loss to know what."

They had been talking as they walked from the car park to the hotel and were now inside.

"Let's meet when we've both showered." Dag suggested.

Opposite, and less than 50 meters along the road from the office block where the Nagaban Consulate was, and only a short distance further away from the door to the Ikebage Embassy was a mini supermarket. At the end of the road about another 25 meters away was a corner cafe and bakery. Dag thought both places were ideal to keep an eye on both of them. They had no intention of being subtle about it, but could still take turns, having a break from browsing obviously outside the mini market and taking a seat in the café's window. Although there were a few benches and shelf tables outside which they could sit at as long as the weather didn't deteriorate.

Dag was first to spend time at the mini market. So obvious was he, that the manager asked him what he was up to, thinking he might be a shoplifter. Dag made a point of showing the woman his ID, and she left him alone. But to anyone watching him, he would stick out like a sore thumb. So much so that Dag was certain they would not think he was a Government or Police agent; they would not be so amateur.

He was right. Only five minutes later a police car came slowly to a halt only meters from him. Two officers got out and strolled over to him.

To an outside observer he was questioned, documentation was checked, questioned again, and apparently told to move on. Dag obliged them, but only a few minutes later Finn was hanging around the mini market.

Dag waited outside the cafe to see if this elicited a response.

There was no police car this time. A large suited man came out of the Consulate door and walked over to the shop. He went in brushing past Finn to get a good look at him. Dag moved. He couldn't leave Finn on his own.

By the time the man had bought an item in the shop Dag was at Finn's side. The man was tall. He was heavily built, and it was muscle, not fat, that strained against the seams of his suit. Dag simply smiled and nodded at him, grabbed Finn's arm and pulled him away walking back to the cafe. They looked back when they got tot he outside bench. The continued to silently watch them. Dag sat the finish the coffee he'd left on the shelf, and Finn joined him. The man waited a few moments longer then walked back to the consulate door. He gave them one more stare before he went inside.

"I expect they photographed everything form an upstairs window." Dag said. "And I'm pretty sure he had a button hole camera to take a close up of us. That should stir things up a bit."

They waited.

They had to order more coffee and cake.

It began to spit with rain, and they were just about to go inside and get as good a seat as they could in the window, when the consulate door opened.

Safia stepped out. Behind her came the guard. They turned away from Dag and Finn and walked North towards the Parliament building just a few hundred meters further on. But they hadn't gone far when, from another doorway, the Ikebage Embassy office building, out stepped the aide to the Brigadier. He followed followed them a few meters behind.

"Now," Said Dag, "that's not a coincidence. Let's follow at a distance."

Leaving their newly purchased coffee and cake they set off.

At the first crossroads Safia and her guard walk on but the

Aide turned right. At the second crossroads, by a square to the side of the Parliament, Safia's guard turned right, but she kept going.

"They're getting us in a pincer movement." Dag explained.

"What shall we do?" Finn asked him sounding worried.

"They won't do anything out in the open. But we won't follow her. We'll cut across the square. The aide is the one who's going to see us do that, but there're two of us and one of him."

Dag thought he heard Finn breath a sigh of relief. "If we come around the back of the Parliament we'll almost be at the Grand Hotel."

"And we can find a spot to watch them meet up there, because I'm sure that's where they're heading. I think we would have been persuaded to go and meet the Brigadier if we'd been surrounded by them."

"There's a lot of people about. Do you think they would have tried that?"

"They would have found some way to persuade us I'm sure."

In the square, at one corner, were some evergreen bushes. Dag and Finn placed themselves behind them as bets they could. He looked back and saw the aide walking across the diagonal of the square heading to the hotel.

"Well, he's not going to confront us on his own." Dag concluded.

Finn pulled Dag's arm. "There's Safia and behind her that guard."

They were walking along the pavement on the other side of the road to them heading for the hotel entrance. The guard was clearly looking around trying to spot them. In moments all three had gone inside.

"That did the trick." Dag said, satisfied. "Let's go for a drink."

"What in the hotel?"

"Yes, why not."

They had hardly had one taste of their drinks when the aide came from the lift into reception. He looked around and immediately spotted them in the bar. He came briskly over and, without asking, took a third seat at the table.

Dag smiled. "Good afternoon." He said brightly.

"Who are you? Why do you spy on us?" He demanded in English.

Luckily Dag's English was pretty good after his spell in London.

"Spying? I don't think anyone would call it spying. We were quite open about it." Dag retorted, still with a smile.

"Then you follow us and watch us. Why?"

Finn was looking from one to the other listening very carefully, interpreting what they were saying.

"We were worried about your safety. We wanted to make sure nothing bad happened to you."

The aide gave a snort. "Bad? Happen to us? What have you heard?" He asked more earnestly at the end.

"Whatever it is I'm sure they are just rumours, Nothing to worry yourself about."

"You will tell me what rumours." The aide demanded.

Dag changed tack. "You seem very close to a member of the Nagamban Consulate, Ms Mesay. Is that unusual."

The aide paused a moment. "Our countries are close. We have close ties. We work together on many things."

"Plans for the future perhaps?" Dag prodded.

"I do not know what you mean."

Again Dag changed tack. "Has Ms Mesay lost anything recently? If she has, I think I know someone who may be able to return it."

The aide frowned and his eyes narrowed. "I do not know what you mean."

"Then maybe you could ask Ms Mesay. If she's interested, we won't be far away. She can contact us."

The aide sat and stared at Dag for a long few seconds, then he stood.

"If I see her, I will pass on your message." He said, turned *and left.*

"If *he sees her.*" *Dag muttered.* "*He knows we know that she's up in the Brigadiers room. Did you get all that?*" *Dag turned and asked Finn.*

"I think so. I watched loads of English and American TV and films. My English is pretty good. But why did you let him know about the map? Won't they come after it, or rather us?"

Dag shrugged. "There's no point just following them. We're not going to learn anything very fast that way. The only way is to throw out the fishing line and see what we catch. But, let's not hang around here. Best get back to our hotel and I'll let Rolf and Randi know what's happened."

It was Randi who got back to Dag.

"Are you sure you did the right thing?" She asked. "You could be putting yourself in danger."

"I thought that was what you wanted – or maybe it was Ingrid? I can't be sure which one of you wants what."

There was a fleeting silence from Randi, a quiet that might have been the signal but could also have been involuntary.

"We have no wish to put you or Finn in danger Dag. Not that I can say the same for Ingrid of course. But I would agree that this is the way to discover what is behind that map. All I will say is – be careful. These are the sort of people who would not hesitate to do something against our laws but would escape justice using diplomatic immunity."

"Don't worry, I'll be careful. And I have no intention of expose Finn in any unnecessary risks."

"Very good. Well, keep in touch. Don't worry too much. We have some operatives not too far away, they can be activated quickly if need be."

It was only minutes later that Dag spoke to Ingrid. The conversation was almost identical to that with Randi, except there was no offer of nearby support. He was on his own as far as she was concerned.

After the phone calls, Fin asked what they were going to do next. Were they going to stake out Safia's apartment again? Dag told him that he didn't think there was much point, and anyway, he could do with a proper night's sleep. They would sit back now and let things take their own course.

"OK." Said Finn. "But I'm going to meet Kenneth, you know, the guy who works at the council. We're going for a drink, maybe a club."

"OK, fine. Ask him if he's heard anything else. And be careful. Keep your eyes peeled. I don't think our Brigadier's people will try anything, but you never know. Any problems, call me straight away. Do you understand?"

"Yes, dad." Finn smiled, and Dag returned a broad grin.

15.

Dag couldn't get to sleep. His mind kept turning over reasons why he had got himself involved in the way he had. Yes, Rolf has asked him to, and yes, he would have helped anyway if Rolf asked. But he still couldn't work out Ingrid's involvement and why Rolf had accepted it. There would have been a reason why it benefited Rolf, and obviously from Ingrid's point of view it must have benefited her. But why use him? They could have simply agreed to work together if it really was necessary; a truce between Rolf and whoever Ingrid worked for on this particular occasion. Both parties wanted to see a particular outcome. But in some way neither wanted to be the architects of the inquiry; Dag, through the unexpected discovery of the map, had become their useful conduit.

He decided he must look more closely at the two countries and their histories; Ikebaje and Nagamba. The reason for Rolf and Ingrid, and whoever she represented, working together, must lie in the politics of the two nations. And, not forgetting, the upcoming Peace Prize ceremony for President Rakha. But, therein lay another puzzle. The prize was now being questioned, not only here in Scandinavia, but around the world. The peace he had brought was breaking down. Some atrocities were said to have occurred with both sides, and both neighbouring nations, blaming the other, and the Brigadier himself had been accused of being involved. But why then was he apparently working so closely with Nagamba, using Safia Mesay as some sort of go-between.

Perhaps they were acting in conjunction against President Rakha. But the Brigadier was his brother-in-law. Not that that might stop him, it never had in many other developing countries. If that was the case, then neither Norway, and probably Sweden, together with whomever Ingrid worked for, wanted that to happen. Or maybe they did. Maybe this involvement may look they they tried even if they failed, and they could wash their hands of it both blaming the other and ultimately pointing the finger at him.

Dag sighed and looked at the clock beside his bed. It was all supposition and questions. He needed to do some research.

He closed his eyes just as his phone pinged. It lit up. There was a message, 'back safely', from Finn. It was nearly three in the morning. Dag gave another sigh, this time of relief, and knew that he could now get to sleep. It was not just the job that was keeping him awake, it was worrying about Finn.

Dag made breakfast but left Finn asleep in his room. In his own room he got out his laptop and began to research the two countries, the President and the Brigadier.

Both were small countries, no bigger than Belgium, and both the remnants of old colonial powers. Hardly anyone noticed their existence except when some catastrophe occurred; whether a famine or less natural disaster, and then the UN usually sent supplies or arranged an African peace-keeping force of sorts. Both countries were Anglophiles, so there was no disparity in international language, but both were split into tribes whose original borders spread across one country or the other, and Christianity still clashed with the old beliefs. Also. In recent years, there had been an upsurge in evangelical Christian churches leading to a fall in in traditional memberships. Throughout the years until Rakha became President, Ikebaje in particular had been riven by squabbles between the different tribes.

President Rakha was of a minority tribe and had surprised everyone by winning an election, which he consolidated more recently in a new one. He had been surprisingly successful until recently at keeping the various sides from splintering the Government and the inevitable collapse, hence his nomination for the Peace Prize. Although, admittedly, there were few other candidates this year.

Dag searched for the Brigadier. His father was the Chief of one of the largest tribal clans which spread over the borders of the two countries, although the greater number of them were in Ikebaje. As Chief, his father had control over a small garnet mine at which they had recently discovered sapphires. It had brought the family considerable wealth. Malidi Jata went to school in the UK and later ,his army training was at Sandhurst; pretty typical stuff for the son of a wealthy member of an ex colonial state. There was nothing much else about him online except a press release of his marriage to President Rakha's sister which had caused a bit of a stir as it was. In a way, the joining of two tribes who had previously always been at loggerheads. One more story popped up just as Dag was finishing. Jata had just been named General Secretary of the ruling political party.

He had become powerful. Powerful enough, thought Dag, that he might unseat the President, brother-in-law or not.

It was half-past ten when Finn knocked on his door.

"What are we doing today?" Finn asked.

"Well, it's a bit late to follow Safia. But I think we'll still take a stroll down the Embassy road, just to make a point. We've thrown out the fishing line and mentioned the map, let's see what happens."

They didn't have to wait long, and they didn't get as far as the Embassy. They crossed the square outside the hotel and headed towards the usual cafe along Prinsens Gate. They where not more than 25 meters away from it when a car pulled up just ahead of them. The two side doors swung open and from the front door the aide came out. He held the door open between himself and them.

"Please get, in." The aide ordered.

It was broad daylight. Dag didn't think they would have taken such a chance in causing a disturbance on the streets of the city, but they seemed perfectly at ease with doing so. They oozed confidence but Dag decided to call their bluff, if it was one.

"No thanks. We're not in need of a lift." He told the aide.

A head appeared out of the back door, then a body. It was Safia.

"It is OK."She told the aide. "I will speak to them." Then, turned to Dag. "But not here on the street."

"If you fancy a coffee we were just going to the cafe there. Why don't you join us?" Dag offered.

She looked at Dag and considered it. "Very well." "You may go. I will be safe." She told the aide.

"What have you done with the map?" She asked as soon as they were sat with coffees.

"Was it you who tried to kill us?" Dag countered.

"Kill you? What do you mean?"

"A car tried to run us over a few nights ago. I assumed it must have been you or you other colleagues."

She shook her head and frowned. "We did no such thing. Not that I know anyway. Now, back to the map."

"The map is the point. It is the only reason someone would have wanted to run us over. And you are the only person that fits."

"I am sorry, you are wrong. I repeat, what has happened to the map?" She insisted.

"I passed it to the police. They must have it." Dag told her.

Safia's eyes narrowed. "You do not lie to me? You gave it to the police."

"Yes, and that is as true as you telling me that you had no hand in trying to run us over."

"If that is so, why do you follow me? You are no ordinary man, Mr Meldel, we have checked. And you say that all you did is hand the map to your police? I find that hard to believe."

"I ask, why do you follow me? Who do you work for?"

"I am working on my own behalf. You have found out that I used to be a detective. Well, that map intrigued me, I thought I'd try to find out more about it."

Safia gave a snort. "If you work on your own how did you find out who I was? You could not do that on your own."

"I admit I had help. Finn here is very good with computers and he has a friend who could help with some security cameras. We managed to track you down."

Safia stood. "I do not believe you Mr Meldel. We just wanted to know who you worked for. If, as you say, you work for yourself, your position is very dangerous. If I were you I would stop any more investigations. If you do not, my friends will act, and it will not be car next time."

With that she turned and left the cafe.

"They're confused. They're not sure how to act. Maybe I

went a bit far in persuaded her that I worked for myself, although I don't think she really believed it. At least it means that they still can't be sure who I do work for. Mind you, that's not to say they may not act as she said they might."

"Do you think they will? Act that is." Finn asked, anxiously.

Dag sipped the remains of his coffee. "I thought they already had, with that car. But now I think it wasn't them. She may have been telling the truth."

"Then who was it?"

"Good question. And I don't have the answer. But the only other two options are either Rolf's people or Ingrid's, and of the two I'd bet on Ingrid. even though she denied it."

"Just as a way to get us involved?" Finn suggested.

"Maybe." Dag pondered. "The other thing that's interesting is Safia herself. She might appear to be just a minor functionary in the Nagamban Consulate – in fact she's supposed to be stationed in Copenhagen, not here in Oslo – but it's her who is taking the lead, when you'd have thought it would be someone from the Ikebaje Embassy. Nagamba's involvement with the Brigadier is much closer than it should be, as is Safia's closeness to him. I think it's clear now that the Brigadier is involved in overthrowing, or at least, destroying the reputation of, the President. It's just a matter of how much official help Nagamba is giving him. We can't be sure though that Safia is working on an official basis."

"But whatever they're planning still doesn't make sense. The Prize-giving ceremony is at the university not the City Hall.

So it can't be that." Finn concluded.

"Kenneth didn't have have anything more for us, then?" Dag asked.

"No, nothing."

Dag looked out of the wall sized window at people passing by. Finn fell silent as well.

Eventually Dag spoke.

"I think we've done what we can. I can't see what else we can do. Safia isn't going to tell us, is she now? If Ingrid and Rolf want to go any further with it, they'll have to do so themselves. I was struggling with why I got myself, sorry us, into this in the first place. I suppose it was the old detective in me. No, enough is enough, and anyway, I want to get to the bottom of our friend Jorgen Lageson. Then, I can go home."

"What do you think you can do about Pastor Lageson? You said yourself that there was nothing which would stand up in court. And what about me? What am I supposed to do?"

"You wanted to come to Kristiansund with me didn't you? You can still do that. As far as the Pastor is concerned, there may still be something in his background that we can get him on. I mean, if we can discredit him, it would stop his mendacious teachings."

Finn shook his head. "They'll still believe in him. They'll accuse you of spreading lies and disinformation, just like Trump. Keep telling falsehoods for long enough and people believe them. It's a fact. They'll get away with it one way or another."

"That doesn't mean we shouldn't try. If no-one tried to oppose such people, where would that lead? They would win. Lies would be perceived as truth, and in the end belief in reality would fade; we would be left with nothing but lies. So, we must try."

"So, where do you start?"

"We got some details from Rolf. We need to look into them more deeply. But first I'd better let Rolf know that I've had enough; and Ingrid too."

After he sent a text to them both Rolf replied almost immediately and asked to meet. Dag waited for a reply from Ingrid but after half an hour or so got none. There was no need to move from the cafe; Rolf was coming there.

"And have you told Ingrid?" Rolf asked Dag

"Yes, but no reply as yet."

Rolf looked at his own coffee and thought for a moment. He looked up and nodded. "Yes, you're probably right. But I'm not sure how Ingrid may take it. When you speak to her, I'd like you to make it clear that this is your decision we have not pressured you in any way."

"Fair enough. I still don't really understand my involvement anyway. Oh, I know I found that map, but it needn't have got me any more involved."

"It was useful to us. Especially to see what Ingrid was up to and who she was working for. We're still not entirely sure of either question. She's got a great knack of losing our tails. And as far as the Brigadier and Safia Mesay are concerned – we had our doubts about them and I think you've pretty much uncovered what they may be up to, but it still doesn't gel. I'm sure there's more to it than meets the eye. But, "Rolf sighed, "the internal affairs of their countries are no affair of ours now, are they? As long as nothing happens on our soil."

"But surely the Government still favours the President?" Finn inquired.

"The Government favours stability. But there again, so do whoever Ingrid works for. Whatever is going on does not seem to be in the interests of either side – whoever the other side is, that is. So, we can only imagine that a third party or parties are involved, but have no idea presently who they are, or what there reasons may be."

"The precious stone mines?" Dag suggested.

"They're valuable, but not remarkably so. Not enough for most other significant powers to have an interest in them."

"Then it must be personal." Dag deduced.

Rolf gave a slight nod as acknowledgement. "Which leaves us with the Brigadier. He's the most likely suspect, but almost too obvious. Not that that would stop him. The only other interesting thing we've dug up about him recently is that he's become a religious convert. Joined one of those evangelical churches which have grown dramatically in recent years. Probably found it useful somehow in getting supporters."

"An evangelical church?" Dag asked.

"Yes, the African Church of the Christian Testament, or some such thing."

Dag stared at Rolf.

"What is it?" Rolf asked.

"Something odd that's all. Something co-incidental; well, almost."

Rolf waited. "Well?"

"It's just that the pastor I asked you to look into for me, Jorgen Lageson, his church is what you might call evangelical, and it has a very similar name, The Church of Christ's Testament."

"Hmm, a similar name I grant you. But I can't see how there could be a connection. Most of these Evangelical Christian churches have similar names, there's not an endless variety of names they can use."

"There's no way the two can be the related." Finn interrupted. "I mean the odds would make it just about impossible. And I'd have heard if there was any connection, I'm sure I would."

Dag and Rolf looked at Finn and then back to each other.

"I'll see what I can find out." Rolf told Dag.

Dag's phoned pinged.

"Oh, here goes, I'll have to meet Ingrid next I suppose."

"I'll leave you to it." Rolf said, as he put on his coat, nodded to Finn, and left them.

Dag waited for Rolf to leave.

"So, are we going to see Ingrid?" Finn asked.

"It wasn't Ingrid." Dag said, surprising Finn. "Safia has got hold of my phone number; everyone seems to be able to."

"What does she want?" Finn asked when Dag failed to continue.

"It's Sunday tomorrow isn't it?" Dag retorted.

"Yes." Finn asked asked, frowning. "So what?"

"She's suggested that we go to church."

"Church? Why? What church?"

"Somewhere where we will learn something to our advantage."

"OK, but where? And why is she telling us?"

"Why she's telling us is what I'd very much like to know. Where – well that's even more interesting. She's suggested we go to a service at The Church of Christ's Testament."

"My church? Why? Why would she send us there?"

"Coincidence, Finn, coincidence. I wonder if there is any such thing. After all, everything is tied, somehow, to everything else in some way or another; cause and effect. You said it wasn't possible. That's never quite true. Things are only highly improbable, but never impossible. It was once said that, given infinity, even that which was considered to be impossible became probable no matter how improbable. All you needed was enough time. And with infinite time all things are probable."

"But how could the Church be involved in all this? It doesn't make sense." Finn said.

"It's something to do with the evangelical movement, at least that which Lageson may be part of. Maybe the similar names of the Churches here and in Ikebaje were also not a coincidence." Dag explained. "The odd thing for the moment is that I haven't heard from Ingrid."

16.

On Sunday morning Dag was up early. He had still not heard from Ingrid. He had kept the car on rental, so they wouldn't have to take public transport to the Church. He had been kept awake that night wondering what Safia had meant by learning something to their advantage, and why he still hadn't heard from Ingrid. Maybe, something had happened to her. If so, Rolf gave no indication of knowing the night before.

As Dag was finishing his breakfast Finn came into the dining room for his.

"I'll go with you, of course," Finn told him, "but I've thought about it over-night and I don't want to go in. I don't want to see my father. Mind you, I wouldn't mind seeing Anette, but not sure if she'd want to see me. Whatever dad says goes as far as she's concerned. If it's all right with you, I'll stay outside."

"No problem. "Dag agreed. "In fact I think it's better you did. You can stay in the car and act as a lookout. Check out anyone going in and out of the Church, or maybe anyone else keeping a lookout. It wouldn't surprise me. After all, Rolf's guys may still be close by, and Safia or the Brigadier's aide might be around, not to mention Ingrid, whatever's happened to her. I'll go in and see what I can discover about this 'something to our advantage'."

Dag looked at his watch. I'll let you finish your breakfast then meet you in reception.

It didn't take long to get to the Church, the roads were quiet on a Sunday morning. They arrived twenty minutes before the service was due to start, parked in a position far enough away not to draw attention but close enough to watch what was going on. Dag remained in the car for most of it. Finn and Dag watched Finn's father go in along with the other worshippers.

He was just about to get out when a taxi drew up outside the Church. A woman got out. The cab drove away. The woman looked around before she went in.

Dag and Finn were left amazed and puzzled. Ingrid had got out of the taxi and gone into the church.

"What the hell's going on?" Dag asked, not expecting any reply. "What is she doing here, and more than that, how could Safia know?" Dag paused, his mind turning it over. "Well, there's only one way to find out. I'm going in. Watch out for me as I come out." He told Finn. "I'll catch Ingrid and speak to her then. Watch my back."

"OK. Don't worry, I'll be here." Finn told him.

There were only high level windows to let the outside light in, but there plenty of strip lights as well, so the Church was bright.

Dag went in just after everyone else had filed through the door and took a seat at the back. No-on had seemed to take any notice of him. He had spotted Ingrid as soon as he had gone in. She too had taken a seat near the back, and Dag had made sure he was a row behind her and out of view.

Maybe, he thought, she was just investigating the Church because of her suspicions about it. But why would she have any suspicions, how would she have found any link between this Church, the map, and the rest of the unlikely links? And how would Safia know about Ingrid and any possible links? He began to feel that everyone knew more than he did.

Lageson began his preaching.

Dag could see that Ingrid was taking in everyone in the congregation. Perhaps she was looking for someone.

Lageson's preaching began with extracts from the bible. Dag tried to listen but the text were old-fashioned language. But two of the extracts stood out.

Then shall they cry unto Jehovah, but he will not answer them; yea, he will hide his face from them at that time, according as they have wrought evil in their doings. Thus saith Jehovah concerning the prophets that make my people to err; that bite with their teeth, and cry, Peace; and whoso putteth not into their mouths, they even prepare war against him.

Then said I, Ah, Lord Jehovah! surely thou hast greatly deceived this people and Jerusalem, saying, Ye shall have peace; whereas the sword reacheth unto the life. At that time shall it be said to this people and to Jerusalem, A hot wind from the bare heights in the wilderness toward the daughter of my people, not to winnow, nor to cleanse; a full wind from these shall come for me: now will I also utter judgements against them.

Each one seemed to have been relating to peace, but Dag didn't have time to think to deeply about them. He would have to try and find out which part of the bible they came from to be able to work out a clear meaning.

He didn't have to do that. Lageson did it for him.

His main points were that false prophets had made people err, stray from the righteous path, and that even as these prophets talk of peace they fight a war against God. And further, that the time has come for the false prophets to face their judgement day.

The statement was clear.

Dag knew that Lageson must somehow be linked to the Presidents Peace prize, and it was certainly not one of support, more likely some revenge was planned for the President receiving it.

Before the end he saw Ingrid move. She was about to get up. Dag ducked down behind the back of the chair in front pretending to see to his shoelaces.

He waited until he had seen her legs go past him and heard the door gently open and close. He waited a few more seconds and then got up and sneaked out as quietly as he could, quietly opening the door. He peered into the open air and looked for Ingrid.

He didn't spot her. He looked farther to where the car was. He couldn't see Finn in the front of the car but it was difficult to tell as the sun was reflecting off the windscreen. He wandered a few meters from the church door and took another look around. He still couldn't see her. Perhaps he had left it too long before following her. He walked over to the car.

Finn was not there.

Dag looked about. Nobody was around. There were no people, no cars. He was feeling a sense of rising panic. He must keep calm. There was probably an innocent explanation. Perhaps Finn just needed to go to the toilet. He opened the car door and looked inside. There was a half-eaten sandwich on the opposite. Finn had brought it with him, but there were no signs of a disturbance.

Dag stood by the car took out his phone. If Finn was anywhere nearby and not in danger, he would answer.

Dag could hear the ring-tone on his phone. But he heard it as an echo. A phone was ringing nearby. He took his away from his ear and listened. It came from the car.

Dag thrust his head inside. The ringing came from beneath the seat. He put his under it. He could feel the buzzing. His hand clasped the phone and he pulled it out.

The phones went into 'leave a message' mode.

Dag disconnected the phones.

He stood back, then walked slowly around the car. Again there was no obvious sign of a disturbance or struggle.

He looked back at the church. He thought he saw a movement. The second door, the one that led to Lagesons' office appeared to swing slightly in the breeze. It was open, left unlocked. Well, either that or someone had opened it. Dag headed straight for it.

He paused in front of the door. He put a couple of fingers to it and eased it gently open a few centimetres. The corridor beyond was dark, there were no lights on, but he could see a narrow crack of light coming from the office door. He listened but couldn't hear anything. The only thing he could do was go in.

He walked gingerly along the corridor towards Lageson's office. He stopped half-way. He had heard a noise from the office. It sounded like drawers opening. Someone was searching the office. He moved forward. Then, he thought he heard whispered voices.

He came to the door. He listened again and heard rummaging. The door was unlocked and also ajar by a slim crack. He pushed it gently with a finger and it moved giving him a bigger crack to through.

He saw the edge of someone. He recognised the clothes. It was Ingrid. She had broke into the office. But he had heard whispering. Someone else must be with her. He gave the door another very gentle push and moved his head to see more of the office.

He was angry.

Without caring for the noise he slammed the door open.

"What the hell's going on?" He demanded.

Ingrid jumped round to face him. Randi spun around and almost fell over a chair.

"What's going on?" Randi retorted. "What are you doing here?"

"Where's Finn?" Dag asked angrily.

"Finn?" Randi asked, puzzled. "Finn. I don;'t know what you mean. Isn't he with you?"

"No he's not. He vanished. From right outside this Church." Dag told her.

Randi looked at Ingrid. "We'd better get out, he'll be back soon. And Dag, you'd better tell us what you're doing here, and what's this about Finn disappearing."

They carefully locked the doors behind them and got to Dag's car just in time as people were coming out from the service.

"He was here. In the car. I went inside to hear the sermon. He was just supposed to keep watch. When I got back, he was gone." Dag explained. "And no signs of a struggle."

"Well, that's one good thing. But why did you come here anyway." Randi asked him.

"We had a message, from Safia. She said we'd learn something to our advantage."

"It looks like it was to their advantage." Ingrid concluded. "Seems Finn has been abducted."

"And pretty obvious who's done it." Said Dag. "You'll have to do something about this." He told Randi.

"I'll get on to Rolf now." She told him and moved away to make the call. "You two get in the car, you're a bit obvious standing there."

They did as they were told.

When she finished the call she got into a rear seat.

"He's putting out a call. But with no description of a car it won't be much use. Not unless they used the Embassy car, but that's got diplomatic immunity. We'd best get back into town."

Dag didn't waste any time getting going.

"Now it's time for you explanations." He told them. "What were you up to and why were you at it together?"

"You were backing out, you said you'd had enough." Randi explained. "We decided it was best if we worked together. It was you who gave us the tip about the Church. We made some further investigations and decided that a deeper look into its affairs was needed."

"That sermon of his was interesting." Ingrid said. "What did you make of it Dag?"

Dag told her. It all sounded like a polemic against those whom we think were advancing peace but their intentions were not actually peaceful. It sounded very much like threat against the Peace Prize.

Ingrid and Randi agreed.

"But, if he is involved, how is he?" Randi asked. "That map was not of the right place. The ceremony is at the University, not the City Hall. So, what is the plan? Is it to disrupt it? Or will it be a direct attack on the President of Ikebaje? But, if so, as I said, what does the map mean?"

"It's all very well and good talking about motives and intentions, but what about Finn?" Dag asked.

"If they've taken him. And that could or couldn't be the Ikebageans. It might be the Nagambans. What do they hope to achieve? Well, keeping you out of their hair, Dag. If it's just to stop you putting your nose into their business, he should be OK." Randi told him. "But, if he's in the Embassy, we can't go in and get him out. It would cause an international incident. Mind you, if it's the Nagambans, theirs is only a consulate, so we might have some elbow room."

Dag parked the car by the hotel. In the foyer, Rolf was waiting for them.

"We've no reports of the Embassy car." Rolf told them. "Not

181

a surprise, any car could have been used. We're checking out the cameras closest to the church, but they're some distance away. Sorry, Dag. But, if they went to the Embassy we might get them on a camera at the end of the road. We're also checking the Grand Hotel where Brigadier Jata is staying."

"I'd start at the hotel." Dag said. "It's not got any immunity, has it? What 'diplomatic' questions can you put to them?" Dag asked him.

"The hotel doesn't, no, but the Brigadier still has immunity and isn't required to answer any of our questions without the approval of his Government, i.e. his President." Rolf told him.

"Safia must have set the trap." Ingrid interjected. "She may be the one to concentrate on. I'm sure I could get her to talk."

"Same problem, she works for the Nagamban Consulate, and I don't think the Government wants an incident with them either."

"But I'm not your Government." Ingrid smiled. "Neither is Dag, not really."

"Hmm. Dag has an ID. He'd have to give it back to me. Then whatever you do we can deny any involvement. I'll leave it to you. I don't want to know the details. But, of course, I'd like to know the results." Rolf said.

"So," Ingrid said, satisfied. "Let's see if we can find Safia."

Dag was uneasy about it. To him Ingrid has been the enemy. Now, he not only had to work for her in a sense, he was now having to to work with her, side by side.

"I've already staked out her address I know where she lives." Dag told her.

"Have you?" Ingrid said cautiously. "Well, I don't suppose she will be working on a Sunday, unless of course she's gone to Church. Let's check her place out."

"We'll call if we get any news." Rolf told them as he and Randi were leaving.

Dag parked the car.

"Let's get in there." Said Dag. "There's no point hanging around outside on the chance of seeing her. Let's see if she's home."

Ingrid nodded. "OK, I'm with you."

Dag didn't press Safia's bell but another one. He blagged his way in saying he was from the police. He still had the voice and authority to get away with it.

He rang Safia's door bell. They waited. He rang it again. There was no reply and not sound came from inside.

"Fancy a look inside?" Ingrid asked, whilst taking a set of small lock picking tools from her coat pocket.

"Always go around with those?" Dag asked.

"I never know when you may need them."

"At the Church office. Of course."

She took her time, then the lock clicked and she turned the door handle.

They were in. The smell was of some exotic cooking. The first room they looked into was the bedroom, clothes scattered untidily over the bed. The bathroom looked as any female only bathroom might look as far as Dag could tell. The lounge was sparsely furnished but tidier than the bedroom. The kitchen had pots, pans, and plates stacked on a draining board, but it was clean.

Ingrid went to take a closer look in the bedroom, Dag concentrated on the lounge. There was a cabinet with drawers which he opened, but they were empty. After all, Safia had not been there long. There was nothing else left out of any interest. Next he checked out the bins, both in the lounge and kitchen. Again nothing.

Ingrid came back successfully holding a laptop in her hands.

"This is about it." She said.

"I've not found anything." Dag told her. "It'll have a password."

"I'll turn it on anyway."

Ingrid sat down on the sofa with the laptop and Dag looked out of the window.

"Shit. She's coming." Dag announced.

"Good, then we'll wait for to tell us the password." Ingrid smiled.

Safia noticed nothing when she got to her door. She opened it as normal and went in to her apartment. She hung her coat on a hanger in the corridor and went into the lounge.

She stopped in her tracks. Sat on the sofa were Dag and Ingrid.

"Do come in." Said Ingrid. "We've been waiting for you."

"What you doing here? You break into my flat!"

"What have you done with Finn, my nephew?" Dag asked, wanting to come straight to the point.

Safia's face was blank. "Who? What you mean, Finn?"

"The young man who was with me. You saw him before. Where is he? What have your people done to him?" Dag explained.

"I do not know what you mean. I have done nothing. You have no right to be here. You break into my flat. You leave. Now!" She demanded, angrily.

"Where have you been today? Where have you just come from?" Ingrid asked.

"It is Sunday. I have been to church." Safia told her.

"And which church might that be?" Ingrid asked.

"I go to the Methodist Church. It is on St Olav's Gate. I know nothing of what you say of this Finn. You must leave. You have no right to be here. I am worker for the Consulate, you cannot question me. I will report you. You break into my flat."

Dag and Ingrid looked at each other, then Dag said, "If I found out you have been lying to us, you will regret it." Then, he stood and said to Ingrid, "Let's go."

"What did think? Was she telling the truth?" Ingrid asked him as soon as they were out of the apartment.

"What does my instinct tell me? Unfortunately, yes. Which cuts out the most obvious lead."

"The only other suspect has to be the Brigadier. It's possible he acted without her knowledge, or anyone at the Nagamban Consulate." Ingrid suggested.

"But if the Nagamban's were mixed up in this, she would surely have known what was going on?"

"We're assuming that they are working on this wholly together. What if they're not?"

"The map proves she is involved, and she met Brigadier Java when he arrived at the airport. They're working together all right. Though maybe she's just being used by him and not privy to everything. All we know now is that she probably wasn't directly involved in Finn's disappearance." Dag concluded. "We need to know what Rolf's people have discovered about the Brigadier at the hotel."

"Shall we make our way there?" Ingrid asked.

"No, let's wait in the car for a while, keep an eye on her for a bit longer." Dag told her.

They didn't have to wait long. Safia came out of the apartment only fifteen minutes later. This time she looked cautiously around before setting off. Dag bided his time before starting the car. She would have to walk to the main road, and then she'd probably get a tram or bus into the centre of town, and, Dag was betting, the Grand Hotel.

She was in their sights just before she reached the main road. They were some distance behind her. As she got to the junction, she stopped. Dag drove slowly so as not to catch up with her. At the corner of the side road and main road a car suddenly stopped. Safia ran over to it and jumped in.

"Damn!" Dag exclaimed. "Someone's picked her up."

Safia's car took off towards the centre and Dag put his foot on the accelerator. He got to the junction. He could see her car driving away into the distance. Cars drove passed him and he was unable to pull out immediately.

"We're going to lose her." Ingrid warned him.

"Not if I can help it."

The cars passed and he drove into the main road. They hit a roundabout just before the tram stop, and again he couldn't pull out right away fro the traffic.

"Why is there so much traffic on a Sunday!" Dag complained.

But by now they had lost sight of Safia's car.

Ingrid gave a deep sigh. "We must assume she's gone to the

hotel to see the Brigadier."

"Can you call Rolf and tell him what's happened. If his people are at the hotel they can confirm that she's arrived there. From what I remember, there's no parking near the hotel. We'll have to look down one of the side streets nearby."

He managed to find a space some way down the nearest side street just as Ingrid had a call back from Rolf. His people reported that they had not seen Safia come to the hotel, and anyway, the Brigadier was not in his room. He had left by a service exit only a short time before. They had a car following him.

"There's no point staying parked here then. We need to be updated where they're going. Wherever it is we are going there was well."

"I'll call Rolf again." Said Ingrid.

Ingrid listened to her phone then spoke. "He's done a pretty roundabout route, but he's gone to Pier 3 on the docks. "

Ingrid paused and listened again. Dag waited.

"Looks like he's boarding a boat. It's a tourist one, does lunches on board. Seems like he's just having a Sunday lunch out on the fjord."

"Then why did he use the service entrance?" Dag asked.

"Probably just because Rolf's team had been spotted. Basis precautions. They'll have a thing about being followed after your confrontation with them. Still, we know where he is, so no need to hurry."

"But did they see any other car? Was Safia there as well?"

"You can ask Rolf yourself, he's coming to the hotel. Come on, let's meet him, he might be there by now."

Reluctantly Dag got out of the car and followed her to the hotel. Rolf was in the bar waiting for them.

Rolf didn't think there was any point Dag going to the harbour. He had people there. He couldn't say if Safia had gone aboard as his people didn't get there until after the Brigadier. She would probably have arrived earlier. But, no problem, They were on the boat, they couldn't go anywhere, and when it returned to the pier they would have the answer. For now, there was nothing else they could do.

"Can we be sure no-one saw anything outside the church?" Rolf asked.

"There was no-one around, not a soul. If it wasn't for the church the place would be deserted, it's basically just a small industrial estate." Dag told him.

"So," said Rolf, "there may be some businesses with security cameras?"

"God, I'm stupid!" Dag exclaimed. "I was too shocked about Finn missing. The church itself, It's got security cameras."

"Hmm, that would mean having a word with Lageson, and I don't want to alert him." Rolf frowned. "This might need the use of your services Ingrid. I think a covert op to gain access to the security tapes. You'll have to make sure the place is empty mind. And I can't admit any involvement. It's Sunday and it would take time to get permission for my guys to do it."

"How long is the boat trip?" Ingrid asked.

Rolf looked at his watch. "Another couple of hours."

"And Lageson should have packed up and gone home after the service. Should give is plenty of time." Dag said.

"Well, I'll leave you to it then. Any news I get, I'll pass on." Rolf told them.

The industrial estate was empty. They parked far enough away from the Church that they could see if there was any activity, which there wasn't, unless Lageson was in his office which they doubted.

They walked to the office door keeping and eye out to make sure they were still alone. They first rang the bell but got no answer, and door was locked so they were in luck, Lageson was not there. Then Ingrid did her trick with the lock. They were in the dark corridor. Ingrid has also come prepared with a small torch in her pocket. It seemed to Dag her pockets were a treasure trove of useful items. Ingrid had to work her magic of the office door itself, which was also locked.

Inside they turned the light on. The recording equipment must be somewhere. Dag found it quickly enough in a cabinet set against wall.

"How do we watch what's on it?" Dag asked.

"Good point. He must have used his computer. Look there's some cables."

"And how do you get into his computer?" Dag asked again.

"Hmm, never easy is it."

They both stopped and thought.

"Well, there's only one thing for it." Dag concluded. "We take them away, look at them, then bring them back."

"Risky. But that's how it'll have to be." Agreed Ingrid.

A call to Rolf and then a call back from him and a place was arranged to take a look at the recordings; at the Oslo Police HQ. Randi was there to accompany them to the facility.

They sat in the darkened room in front of a set of three video screens. The recordings were on DVD and Randi slipped them into the slot of a player.

A time date stamp was in the top right-hand corner, and they fast forwarded to the point where Dag and Finn had arrived in the car. The problem was that the cameras were predominately centred on the church doors and only the very periphery of the coverage picked up the car's arrival. When it parked only a small part of the front bumper and hood could be seen. Dag's legs appeared when he left the car, and he only came fully into view when he was very much closer to the door.

They let the DVD play. For a brief second Dag thought he saw another car pass close to his. They rewound and went forward in slow motion, but it was impossible to get anything from it. A few seconds later they saw a pair of feet at Dag's car door. Someone had stopped and apparently talking to Finn. As the feet moved away the car door opened and Finn's feet appeared. Both of them disappeared off-screen. Again some more seconds later, the mystery car drove at the farthest reaches of the picture. It would be impossible to get any identification.

"No struggle, as you said Dag. Seems very strange." Ingrid said.

"And easily persuaded." Randi added. "He went without much of a chat about it."

"There's only one thing it can mean." Dag told them. "He knew who it was, and knew them pretty well, or he wouldn't have left the car."

"Let's do a copy, there's some spare DVD's here. I'll see if our people can get anything extra from it." Randi offered.

Dag nodded, but didn't expect to get any more detail from it. What he had seen was mist peculiar. He had been quite firm with Finn that he mustn't leave the car, and he didn't think Finn would do so unless something very unusual persuaded him to. Who could it be to have so easily persuaded him?

"Wait a moment!" Dag stopped them from copying the discs. "Can we look at them again and see who went into the service?"

They rewound the recording and watched the people turning up for the service. Dag saw himself, then they saw Ingrid going in. They watched.

"Stop." Dag ordered. He had seen his brother-in-law going in. "Go on, slowly." He watched until they saw Lageson opening the door. "He was on his own." Dag said. "Where was his daughter, my niece, Finn's sister. She wasn't there. Why not?"

"You'd better have a chat with your brother-in-law and niece." Randi said.

"Let's copy these discs and get them back first, then we'll go and have a chat with this brother-in-law of yours." Said Ingrid.

They had no problem regaining entry into the Church office and were in and out within minutes. They were lucky, though, as they were driving away a car passed. They slowed to watch it. It parked outside the Church and Lageson got out and went through the door to the office.

"That was a bit of luck." Dag said as he drove off.

"Let's hope it stays with us." Ingrid retorted.

It wasn't far to go to get to Dag's brother-in-law; just an eight-minute drive. They parked a little way down the road. Dag wanted to watch the place for a moment before they went in.

"There's no car parked outside." Ingrid noted.

"No, but then, if it was Anette who persuaded Finn, she must have used another car. Which has got me thinking, she's doesn't drive, she's too young."

"And her father was in the service."

"So, another person is involved. Damn, it's not as straightforward as I thought. I should have taken time to think it through."

"Even so, likely or not, her father will be involved."

"Either that or it has nothing to do with Anette at all, and we've gone down the wrong path. She may not have been at the service for some other reason. Come on then let's go and have a chat." Dag decided.

They rang the doorbell and waited. There was no sound from inside and no-one came to the door. Dag rang it again but expected no answer. No-one came.

"What now?" Ingrid asked.

"We see if Rolf can find out his car registration. He should be able to easily enough. Then, we need the police to put a call out." Dag replied.

Ingrid called Rolf when they were on their way back to the car. As they got to it, a neighbour came out of the house they were parked outside.

"You've missed them." The neighbour told them. "Went off about an hour ago."

"I see." Dag smiled at her. "No idea where they've gone I suppose?"

"What him? No, he doesn't mix much. His wife was nice

though. Shame, that was, her dying so sudden."

"Tell me. Did his children go with with?"

"No. Went on his own. Finn hasn't been around for a while. Don't think he got on with his father. Anette left his morning with a young man in another car."

"Ah, I see, thank you. You would be able to describe the car would you?" Dag asked her.

She frowned and asked suspiciously. "Are you the police?"

"Ex Detective Dag Meldel. Kristine was my sister. I need to talk to Anders and Anette."

"Oh! Kristine mentioned you. Let me think now. I'm not good with cars, they all look the same to me. But it was dark, black probably. It was like that one over there." She pointed to an SUV across the road.

Dag nodded and smiled. "Well, thanks, that's very helpful Mrs ....?"

"Sahlberg, Klara Sahlberg."

"Can you describe the young man?" Dag asked.

"Just a young man. They're a bit like cars these days. All dress and look the same. Jeans, dark jacket, like a ski jacket. Oh, he had red hair; ginger sort of. And glasses. He wore glasses."

"Thanks Mrs Sahlberg, you've been a great help."

In the car, Ingrid said, "Maybe one of her school friends. I wonder if she's got a Facebook page? The pictures they post on it give away all sorts of facts about their lives."

"Finn would have known." Dag said.

"I'll search now, on my phone." Ingrid used her smart phone as they drove back to Dag's hotel. "Can't find her on it at all." She said after a couple of minutes.

"What about the Church? Has it got a web presence?" Dag asked her.

She continued her searching. "Yes, and there're some photos. Let me see." She fell silent for a couple of minutes. "I can see Anders in one but neither Anette nor Finn."

"So, we have the description of a car and its driver." Dag mused.

"And at least one passenger whom we can describe in full." Ingrid reminded him. "Maybe she was running away from home?"

"Perhaps. But Finn said she devoted to her father. A reason he and she didn't get on."

"Still, her heart may have been turned by some young man. It wouldn't be the first time." Ingrid suggested.

"Maybe. But it just doesn't really fit with what I know about her, or at least, what Finn's told me about her. We'll have to tell Rolf what we've found out and see what he can come with."

17.

"Not much to go on as far as your niece is concerned, but we've got Anders' car registration and put a call out, although I've said that he is not to be stopped. I'd sooner find out where he's going and what he's up to first – and if there's anyone else in the car with him." Rolf told Dag and Ingrid when they met up with him.

They'd gone to the hotel, parked the car and then had a call to meet at the usual cafe.

"As far as the Brigadier and Safia are concerned , they've just returned from the Sunday Lunch aboard the boat. They met up with a couple of others from both the Embassy and the Consulate; the Ambassador and the Consul themselves. It looks like it was just a planned meeting between the Country's representatives. So, there's no direct link with them and Finn's disappearance."

"Is it normal for two Country's people to meet up like that?" Dag asked.

"Of course. It's whole point of what they call diplomacy. But you never know what either side is up to, and very often neither side knows what each other's up to either. That's also diplomacy." Rolf explained.

"They're planning something." Ingrid said emphatically.

"Very possibly. If we'd had notification of their meeting we might have arranged to find out. But that opportunity didn't present itself." Rolf told her. "The only thing that can give us some assurance is that it now seems very unlikely that Finn was abducted by either of them. It looks much more like a family affair if you ask me."

Dag shook his head. "It just doesn't fit with what I know about Anette, nor Finn. It must be something to do with Lageson. Anyway, you promised to look into him more carefully. Did you find out anything?"

"Ah, yes. The funding for the Church came from an overseas account. Unfortunately from a Country with very secretive banking systems. The bank itself is used by all sorts of organisations, as well as various presidents and the like of a number of countries. Not that we can find out anything specific. However, I've just found out that President Manasé Rabenarivo of Nagamba is one of their clients, as is the African Church of the Christian Testament. So, there's a connection, even if tenuous."

Dag sat back in his seat. "I need my whiteboard. I want a picture of all this in from of me."

"Has you hotel got a conference room or office we could use?" Ingrid asked.

"An operations base?" Rolf mused.

"I should think they could find us something" Said Dag.

A word from Rolf and it didn't take much persuading for the hotel to give them a room they usually hired out for meetings. Dag also managed to get a whiteboard from the manager. He set in up against the wall of the room with a desk and several chairs facing it.

"So," said Rolf, "Do we start with the map at the top, and Safia?"

"And then the Brigadier and President Rakha." Ingrid suggested.

"Hmm. OK." Agreed Dag, but adding his own name at the top next to the map as well as Safia's. "There's also the aide, of course. What's his name?"

"Captain Fadika." Rolf said.

Dag wrote his name and continued. "Then I contact the Police, then Rolf's involved." He wrote it down. "And, one way or another, you are." He added, writing Ingrid's name next to Rolf's.

"You tell Finn about the map and get him involved." Said

Ingrid.

Dag nodded but said nothing, and added Finn's name beside Ingrid's.

"And that gives us the names of the people I came here originally to see, Anders and my niece Anette." He added their names under Finn's. "And that linked us to Lageson and his church."

Now Lageson's name had been pushed to the right and under the Names of the Brigadier and President Rakha.

"If I add the African Church and link it to the Brigadier," He wrote it under the Brigadier's name and below that of the President. It took a position on the board just above the name of Lageson and his Church.

Dag stood back and mulled it over.

"A question." Dag said. "Ingrid. How and why did you get involved? You have never said, and it's one of the questions that stands out first."

"The people I work for - and I have various clients and different times – had heard that there may be some kind of disruption to the Peace Prize. They are keen to see peace in the region. Any threat to President Rakha would upset their plans. In fact, anything to upset the fragile peace between Ikebaje and Nagamba would be against their interests. It so happens that your country, as well as other European countries, feel the same way. That's why I contacted Rolf's superior. It was easier if we worked together."

"It was you getting your hand on that map which was the strangest coincidence." Said Rolf. "And a timely lead. We both agreed to get you involved. But I have to admit, the coincidence surrounding Finn and Lageson is most extraordinary."

"Just one of those things." Said Dag. "They seem to happen to me all the time. It's that link between the Churches you need to concentrate on, Rolf. We need to know more about them."

"There's nothing there that explains why Finn has gone missing, except his and his family's link to the Church. Does he know more than he's let on? Or do they think he knows more than he should?" Ingrid asked.

"Either." Rolf said. "And to get to the bottom of that, we need to talk to Lageson."

"I'd sooner find Anders first. It's Finn who is my first concern. Give us what you know or any leads and we'll deal with him." Dag told Rolf. "You can concentrate on Lageson and his links to the African Church."

"I'll call now and see if anything has come up." Rolf agreed and went to the back of the room to make it.

"The map still makes no sense." Ingrid said with a frown. "Why the City Hall? The ceremony is at the University."

Dag joined her frown. "There's something missing. I'm sure there is. But I can't put my finger on it."

"Got him!" Rolf informed them. "Anders' car has been spotted. My officer is keeping up surveillance. He's at that Church of his. If Lageson is there as well we can kill two birds with one stone."

"Let me talk to Anders first." Dag advised him. "If we all go blundering in we'll give away the fact that we know more than just the fact that Finn's gone missing. And anyway, if we find Finn then we may discover some of the other answers."

"Not if it's a simple matter that he's help Anette run away from her father and nothing to do with anything else." Ingrid reminded him.

"Let's get a move on anyway. I can hang back with my officer. You can talk to Anders. Will Ingrid go with you?"

"May as well." Dag said. "You can always be my girlfriend!" He joked, looking at her.

"Fat chance." She rebutted him.

Rolf kept in touch with his officer on the way there to make sure Anders hadn't left. Dag parked around the side of an industrial unit out of sight of the Church and Rolf strolled over to his man's car before Dag and Ingrid walked up to the Church.

It was dark now, and the sodium lights of the business park bathed the Church in a lurid glow. The outside door to the office was locked, but the door to the Church was slightly ajar. Dag swung it open and went in with Ingrid behind him.

The Church was quiet, a silence that insinuates itself into such places. The door behind them gave a slow groan as it slowly swung shut. From the empty seats in front facing the platform from where Lageson preached, a head rose up. It was Anders. Dag thought he must have been on his knees, praying. Anders stood, and looked around at them.

"You! Where is Anette? What have you done with her?" Anders demanded.

"Anette? I thought she would be with you. It's Finn I've come about, not Anette." Dag answered. "Where is Finn? Do you know where he is?"

"Finn. Why should I know where he is? He's not been my son since Kristine died. He was taken from me. The devil crept into his heart and seduced him. And you! You are the devil's agent. Why did you come? You took him from me! And now his sister; now Anette as well. What have you done to them?"

Anders came towards them. Ingrid tensed behind Dag. Dag put his hand up.

"That's far enough! No devil has done anything to alter Finns' heart. A man, maybe, but no devil."

"You, you are that man!" Anders said angrily.

"You will know that is not true, if only you looked more deeply into your own heart." Dag retorted. "My only concern now is to find Finn and, if she is with him, Anette. There's no point your casting blame where none exists. The only way we are going to find them is if we work together."

"I have prayed for their return. God will provide the answer. He will bring them back to me."

"I think you will need more help than prayers. Besides that, maybe it was your prayers that brought us here." Dag said, thinking he could turn the argument. "Maybe it is God's will that we came and offered our help. Why then would you deny it? Surely if we are the answer to your prayer, you have to accept our help."

Anders' face flickered in a state of momentary confusion. He was grappling with the argument that Dag had put forward. If he was to refuse their offer of help, it would be tantamount to denying the Lord. For a second or two he felt the torment that St Peter must have felt. God was denied. Should he be as Peter? He could not. But he was no Saint, and he knew it.

Tears seeped from Anders' eyes and slipped slowly down his cheeks. He took a deep breath and swallowed.

"Very well." Said Anders, his shoulders slumping and his voice soft and quavering. He wrung his hands and sat on a nearby chair. "What have I done? What has happened to them?"

Dag took a chair next to him and Ingrid sat further away.

"Tell me, when did you last see her?" Dag asked him.

Anders thought, then said, "Before coming to the Church Service. She said she wasn't feeling well, so I let her stay behind."

"Can I ask you, did she have a boyfriend?"

"No! She didn't. What sort of girl do you think she is?"

"A very normal girl I'd have thought. Most girls her age have a boyfriend even if it's not serious." Dag said.

"Well, she didn't." Anders insisted.

"I'm asking that question because we have already made some enquiries." Dag told him. "A neighbour saw her leave after you went to Church, with a young man, in a car."

Anders frowned and looked angry again. "What young man?"

"I don't know, that's why I asked. And from your answer you're not likely to know either."

"Computer – phone?" Ingrid whispered.

Dag took her hint. "Does Anette have a computer or a mobile phone?" He asked Anders.

Anders looked up. He'd been staring at the floor. "She has a phone. I expect she has it with her. And a computer at home for her homework. They say they all need one these days, but I don't like it."

"And you've tried phoning her?"

"Of course. It's dead, it just asks to leave a message."

"And you left one?"

"What do you think? Of course I did."

"Well. I suggest we go back to your house and see what clues we can pick. And my friend Ingrid here," He held out his and to introduce her, "should be able to help if Anette has a computer."

It was as if Anders had only just realised she was there. He frowned, and asked. "Who is she?"

"Ingrid works for a .. a Government agency. She can help."

"Agency? What sort of agency?" Anders said with suspicion.

"She's just a friend of mine. We've known each other for a long time. She lives here in Oslo, that's why we met. But she's an expert in computers, so she can help us with Anette's computer. Maybe there will be some clues on it."

Anders sighed, and reluctantly agreed.

"By the way," said Dag, "how did you get into the Church?"

Anders pulled a set of keys from his pocket. "I've got a set of keys. I do odd jobs about the place for Pastor Lageson whenever he asks."

"Are they for the office as well?" Dag asked him.

"No just the Church. I don't go into the office unless he lets me."

At Anders' house they entered Anette's bedroom. It looked as if she had tidied and cleaned it scrupulously before she left.

"Does she always leave it this clean?" Dag asked Anders.

"Yes, she's a good girl. She always does as she's told."

Dag gave him a glance. "Not exactly. Or she'd still be here. Can you have a look for her phone, just in case it's still here? At least she's left her laptop on that desk. Ingrid, can you have a look at it?"

"Her phone's not here that I can see." Anders told them.

"Take a look downstairs, will you? We'll work on the computer." Dag told him.

Anders hesitated, but then nodded and left.

"Any luck?" Dag asked Ingrid.

"Password protected. Tried a few obvious ones. What's her birth date?"

Dag had to think but couldn't recall ever knowing it. Luckily when he looked on a calender put on the wall with blue tack, it was marked. Ingrid tried it in various combinations without luck.

"I'm not going to get into it by chance." She told Dag. "We'll have to let Rolf's people do their tricks with it."

As Ingrid had been trying, Dag had scanned the books on Anette's shelf. There was a well-used bible. Dag took it out. A piece of paper was between the pages as a book mark. He opened it and looked at the page. There was a note on the piece of paper; Micah 3:4. He read the verse that had been bookmarked.

Then shall they cry unto Jehovah, but he will not answer them; yea, he will hide his face from them at that time, according as they have wrought evil in their doings. Thus saith Jehovah concerning the prophets that make my people to err; that bite with their teeth, and cry, Peace; and whoso putteth not into their mouths, they even prepare war against him.

It was the verse that Lageson had used in his sermon.

Anders had still not returned from his search of downstairs.

"Ingrid." Dag said. "Try Micah 3:4 as a password, or something like that."

Ingrid typed on the keyboard. And then typed again, and once more.

"Got it!" She exclaimed. "I'm in."

Dag frowned. Where was Anders?

He went to the top of the stairs and called down. "Anders! Have you found her phone?"

Dag listened. There was no reply. He rushed down the stairs to look for Anders.

The lounge and kitchen were both empty. Anders was not there. Dag went outside. Anders car had gone. Dag hadn't heard him drive off, but he was gone.

Dag sent a text to Rolf to tell him and ask him to pick Anders up, then hurried back upstairs.

"He's gone." Dag announced to Ingrid.

"That's a surprise. I didn't really trust him. He's a bit irrational if you ask me. But come and have a look at this."

Dag came behind her to look at the screen.

"This is her browsing history." Ingrid pointed to the list.

"She hasn't cleared it. Here, yesterday, and again this morning." She clicked on the item from that morning. It opened a web page. "The website of the African Church of the Christian Testament."

They both read as Ingrid scrolled down the page. It seemed innocent enough although Dag recognised some of the language as being very similar to that used by Lageson. There was a telephone number, which Dag made a note of, but it would be a local one to the country where it was based.

"Is there an email address?" Dag asked.

"Funnily enough, no. But there's a contact page for more information. It doesn't show the address, but hang on, if I right click a new page will show me the source code."

The page came up. A long list of confusing lines of programming, beyond Dag's knowledge. To save time looking for the email, Ingrid used another trick that Dag had not seen before and did a search of the programme page looking for the 'mailto' word found in an email address. She found it.

"There you go." She said, pointing out the email address which Dag also wrote down in the small notebook he still had the habit of carrying with him. "Now," she added, "Let's see if she has sent an email to that address."

Ingrid got into Anette's email account easily enough, Anette had used the same password as so many people usually do.

"There you go." She said. "I'll just do a search and bring up all the emails for that address."

She got the full list of both incoming and outgoing emails,

and they began to read them.

After a while Dag said, "We'd better get all of this to Rolf. Let's take the laptop."

Ingrid agreed and made a call. Rolf phoned back moments later. He told them to get back to the hotel room they were using. They would examine it in more depth there.

When they got to the hotel Rolf had someone with him. He introduced him just as Torje. Neither Dag nor Ingrid cared to ask exactly who he was or who he worked for; a Government department no doubt, but not Rolf's. He was the one who took the most interest in the computer, and evidently knew what he was doing as he sat at the desk in front of it with his fingers typing nimbly by touch. Dag would have been continually looking at the keyboard even though he had learned type fairly quickly over the years of writing up reports.

"Most interesting." Torje said enigmatically.

"Does it tie in with what you told me earlier?" Rolf asked him.

"It reinforces some of our thoughts." Torje replied. "Not that we had any firm leads. This has given us some to go on. But I think we would consider it more convenient if you led things, seeing as you are in place. It would save time and effort."

"Excuse me." Dag interrupted them. "Can you explain what you're on about?"

"Torje has been involved in a different matter which, it seems, overlaps our investigation." Rolf explained. "He is more interested in what happens on foreign soil, as it were, rather than on our own. There have been further reports this morning of fire-fights on each side of the Ikebaje and Nagamban border. Each side blames the other, of course. But hardly the best publicity just ahead of President Rakha's Peace Prize. It's a matter of who is behind the violence, who is stirring things up, and what they hope to gain from it. The finger has been pointing towards the Brigadier for some time now but with no proof. He still seems to have the President's ear and be a favourite of his, besides being a relative of course. It's this thing about the Church that's interesting; an element that hadn't been taken into account before."

"You're talking about a coup, then." Said Dag.

"Not just a coup." Rolf said. "Coups – plural."

"Both countries." Ingrid broke in.

"Ikebaje and Nagamba." Rolf confirmed. "It's not just President Rakha who is at risk but President Rabenarivo of Nagamba as well."

"And the man who could take over from both of them, uniting both countries," Ingrid concluded, "Brigadier Jata."

"Exactly." Agreed Rolf.

"But what has the Church got to do with it?" Dag asked.

"Funds, initially. Plus, a fervent following." Torje joined in. "How many countries are there in the world where Presidents have found it useful to align themselves with a church and its believers? Even President Putin has become a staunch supporter of the Russian Church. It proves incredibly useful."

"And he already has a good proportion of the shares in the mining companies. I wouldn't be at all surprised if they were nationalised as soon as he takes over. Then, he'll control it all." Ingrid added.

Rolf gave her a look. Dag suddenly understood. Ingrid was not acting for a Government as he had thought, she was being paid by the international mining companies to protect their interests.

"Can we get back to Finn and Anette, and what's on the computer? Can it tell us anything – how to find them?" Dag asked.

"She has been in contact with the African Church, as you know." Torje told him. "But to start with she used a contact page on their website, so it's not immediately apparent what she wrote. It would take a lab to see if they might be able to extract that info. What we do have is her actual emails to them, which she wrote later on after she made contact. One thing is certain, she mentioned her pastor, Lageson, almost from the start. I'm wondering if he might have put her up to it, got her to be in contact with them rather than himself, thereby keeping himself in the clear. Anyway, most of the emails are talking about peace, or at least their perception of what peace means and how to go about procuring it, which doesn't gel with ours."

"Yes, yes." Dag interrupted. "We got the general gist of all that ourselves. Is there anything that gives a hint of where she or Finn might be and what they're up to?"

"What they're up to? A good question. There are some hints. Whoever is writing the emails from the African Church side uses a single name – Tocha. An obvious alias. Portuguese for 'torch' actually, and similar to a number of languages in that area. But I've just run a programme to look a regularly used words. Most are, of course, the one's we use in everyday speech, but the word 'University' crops up more times than it should, as does the word 'hall', and in relation to them, the Ceremony. So, what they are up to is, I would say, linked to the Peace Prize ceremony at the University. They either plan to simply disrupt it, or something much worse. Unfortunately that isn't clear in any of the emails."

"Anette? Finn? I can't really believe that, especially not Finn he has no time for any of that Church nonsense and was angry that his father had induced and indoctrinated her into it." Dag said with confidence.

"Maybe not Finn, no. But Anette is in deeper than even she might realise." Torje said. "I say that because she has forwarded emails to The Church of Christ's Testament, that is, Lageson."

"Has there been any word about him?" Dag asked Rolf.

"Not as yet, no. He's gone to ground it seems. As well as your brother-in-law."

"You'd better update the whiteboard, Dag." Suggested Ingrid. "You can draw a few more connections on it."

Ingrid was right, Dag needed to get a visual idea of it all. He had connected the Churches already, but now drew a line to connect Anette and Lageson directly to the African one, and wrote the name 'Tocha' under the African Church.

"Maybe this Tocha is in Norway?" Rolf mused. "Maybe it was him who picked up Finn. He could have used Anette as some sort of lever."

"Threatened to do something to her if he didn't cooperate?" Ingrid suggested.

"I can't imagine him going along otherwise." said Dag.

"Maybe 'Tocha' is Safia or even the Brigadier?" Ingrid suggested.

"Or anyone else in the African Church or in the Embassy or Consulate here in Oslo." Rolf suggested. "The web could truly be world-wide."

"We'll have to warn the University and the Nobel committee organisers about our suspicions." Said Torje as much to Rolf as the others. "There will have to be extra security measures put in place."

"I'll deal with my end if you deal with yours." Rolf told him. "I need to get back to the office." He told Dag. "As soon as I have any news or leads I'll let you know.

Rolf and Torje left leaving Dag and Ingrid staring at the whiteboard.

"I still feel we're missing something." Dag murmured.

"And still none of it ties in with the map. The map is still the odd thing about it all." Said Ingrid.

There was no further news that night. Ingrid had left Dag still staring at the whiteboard but having no useful thoughts, and he had eventually given up and eaten late dinner alone at a nearby Italian Restaurant, eventually being the last person to leave with the staff clearing up around him.

He knew his mind wouldn't settle, and he'd not get to sleep easily so afterwards decided to go for a drink. He wandered along the streets he had grown use to during the previous days and found himself at the City Hall piazza and the corner pub. It was busy. He ordered a small beer and looked for somewhere to sit. He had to squeeze up against a dry bar in the corner of the room next to a large window that looked out onto the piazza. It was noisy and he couldn't think. He wished now he'd found a quieter place and made up his mind to down the beer and go somewhere else; the whiskey bar he'd found the other day would be a better place.

He gulped down the beer and made to move. It was then he caught sight of two people outside wandering across the piazza. One was Safia, the other the aide to the Brigadier.

Dag made his way to the door, keeping an eye on them as best he could through the crowd of people and available window. By the time he was out of the door they were at the side of the piazza and heading out along the exit road. He hurried to keep them in sight but not too fast to get too close.

He wondered what they had been doing there. Had they been sussing out the piazza and the Council building again? The street was a short one and opened out onto a main road and a public square just along from the Grand Hotel. Maybe, they had just been out for a meal and were heading back there. Or at least the aide would be, but Safia was further from home. They turned right. A little way along the road they stopped. Dag ducked into a doorway but peered out from it to keep them under observation. Safia and the aide talked for a moment, and then went into a building. Dag waited a few seconds before finding out where they had gone into. It didn't take long for him to see that the sign was for a pub. They were having a drink together. Maybe the aide, Captain Fadika, Dag now remembered his name, had to persuade her.

Now he had to make a decision whether to go in or not.

On the other side of the road in the public square some sort of mobile generator had been set up. He decided to use it as cover from where he could stake out the pub and wait for them to leave.

An hour went by and the night was cold with a light fine dusting of snow beginning to fall. Dag was huddled against the generator to keep warm. He looked at his watch; it was 23:35. One hour and four minutes. Then, a car pulled up outside the pub. It was black with tinted windows. It was an angle that prevented Dag seeing the registration number, but he was sure it was blue and not the normal white, and that would mean it was a diplomatic car.

The door of the pub opened. Safia came out first followed by Captain Fadika. The driver got out of the car to open the door. It was the Brigadier's large guard. At first, Dag didn't take notice of the young man who came out of the door just after them. He assumed it was just another customer on his way out. But the man stopped, and Safia and Fadika turned and spoke to him. Safia's and Fadika's faces were turned away from Dag, but he could see the young man who nodded several times and spoke to them.

The young man had reddish ginger hair and wore glasses. This was the man Mrs Sahlberg, Anders' neighbour had described, Dag was sure of it. His camera was in his hand, and he took a picture.

There was a flash. Dag had forgotten that the flash would come on automatically in the darkness. He dived back behind the generator and waited. He counted until he was sure no-one was coming and peered back around the generator. The car had driven off. He looked around for the young man. He saw him. He was not too far away. Dag turned up his collar against the cold and increasing snow and followed him. At the same time he called Ingrid. She didn't answer, so he left a message and told her who he was following.

The young man turned right just passed the Parliament Building. Dag hung back so as not to get to close. The streets were pretty empty now and following the man would be more obvious.

The young man was over half-way down the street and Dag had just begun to move again when a bus went passed him. Dag felt a momentary premonition. The bus pulled up just where the young man had got to. It was a bus stop. Dag began to run, but as soon as his quarry was on the bus it took off. He was too late. Again he had be thwarted by public transport. But he had the number of the bus. It was 54. He wondered where it went. He could call Rolf, and they may be able to catch it or he could find out the route and, if he had time, get the car out of the car park. No, that would be too late. He sent a text to Rolf, then headed back to his hotel.

He had just got to his room when Rolf called. He had sent a car to chase down the bus. They had stopped it and gone on board but the suspect was not on board. The driver believed he had got off at Møllerveien only about 1.5 kilometers from Dag's hotel. The guy had been lucky to catch the bus, it was the last one that night, which suggested he might be a regular user and that the area around Møllerveien was likely to be where he lived.

"Interestingly," Rolf said, "there's quite a number of different churches all grouped around there. But it's very much a residential part, although there is an area with a couple of hotels, restaurants and the odd bar. He could live anywhere around there."

"And Finn and Anette could be there as well." Dag added.

"I'll set up a couple of roving patrols. We had that description of him, and that photo you took, he should stand out. For now I'd get some sleep, I expect he'll be doing the same, wherever he is."

18.

The next morning was clear and bright with a cloudless sky, although Dag was awake and up before the sun had risen. He was the first at breakfast and had already sent a text to Rolf asking if there was any overnight news. There wasn't.

He considered what to do. He didn't like the thought of sitting around the hotel waiting for news. He wanted to do something constructive. The only thing he could think of was to get the car and take a look at the area where Rolf had said the young man had got off the bus, so he checked it out on the map on his phone. There was parking in a side street not far from the bus stop and close to a river bridge and park. He would be able to walk around the area as well as drive around it. He knew there wasn't really much chance of spotting the guy in such a well-built-up area with what looked like many blocks of apartments, but he always believed that, in these circumstances, even a very small chance was worth the effort.

He got to the bus stop within ten minutes of leaving. He was going against the flow of commuter traffic into town. He passed it, turned right at a roundabout then right again and parked the car. He walked to the bus stop and stood at it. It would have been useful if the driver had mentioned which way the young man may have gone after getting off, but Dag didn't suppose he would have taken any notice anyway.

He walked to the roundabout. Across the road he saw a couple of restaurants and takeaways, and crossed over. Maybe, they were open after midnight and the guy had used them. Two were closed, and their window notices said they shut before midnight. The third was bigger, opened until late, and did takeaway food, but it too wouldn't be open until lunchtime. Dag made a note to come back if necessary.

He went back to his car. It was still early and if young people anything to go by it was more than likely that the guy would not be up yet. Unless he had a job, of course.

Dag jumped back out of the car. If he had a job, he may well use the bus to get to work. It was obviously a bus route that took him to where he lived; around here. Dag walked back to the bus stop and saw, further along on the opposite side of the road, the bus stop for journeys into town. Several people were standing at it waiting for a bus, but neither were the young man. Dag decided to remain by his bus stop and keep an eye on it from a distance.

A bus came his way first, and he had to signal to the driver that he didn't want to get on. The driver didn't look impressed.

A minute or so later a bus drove passed him and stopped at the other bus stop. The passengers got on. Just as the doors were closing. From around a nearby corner ran the red-headed young man,. He got to the bus in time to stop the doors closing and jumped aboard.

Dag swore. The guy had come out of a gap between two apartment buildings. Dag ran back to his car. He needed to catch up with the bus; and let Rolf know. In a couple of minutes he was turning on the car engine and setting off. He was at the junction with the main road just a minute later. But that gave the bus a three minute start, the morning traffic had built up, and he didn't know the bus route. Without knowing it he made an error almost at the start. As soon as he'd turned onto the main road he went straight ahead heading directly into town, but the bus route went to the left at a junction directly after him joining the road.

Ahead of him was a long straight stretch of road. He could see all the way along it, but there was no sign of the distinctive bus. He drove on. But not for long. He knew he must have mad a mistake. The bus must have turned off. He remembered the crossroads. The bus would not have turned right away from town, it must have turned left. He had to take the next turning left himself. He reached a wide junction, got into the lane to turn and went left. He drove passed a junction. Ahead was another. He was caught in a line of six or seven cars. At the junction ahead a bus appeared from the left, and turned going in the same direction as him. He had caught up with it. This time he wouldn't lose it.

Each time it stopped he had to stop at the kerbside himself. Each time he set off again behind it.

The bus went left and right at junctions. Dag had not see the young man get off. Soon the bus was stopping the front of the railway station and his hotel. Still Dag did not see him get off. The bus carried on and turned left along the street where he and

Finn had nearly been run over. At the end of the street it turned right and stopped again, opposite the stop where the young man had got on the night before. It was not far from the pub, the Grand Hotel, and the Parliament building. But, he didn't get off at that stop either. The bus continued on,, passed the park where Dag had hidden, then to the end of the public square and the National Theatre.

There, just in front of a roundabout the bus stopped. There was no mistaking the young man who got off. But there was nowhere Dag could pull up, he had to drive on and around the roundabout. The guy was walking back the way the bus had come heading past the National Theatre. In no time Dag would have gone past him. He had to pull over, but there was no stopping on the road, only the pavement.

"He hit the hazard lights and pulled over half way onto it. He needed to watch where the guy was going, and he saw him cross over and carry on walking until he was almost lost amongst people, and then he set off again.

The young man walked beyond the Theatre and back to the end of the public square. Then he turned right. Dag knew the road. It was the one that led up to the City Hall and piazza.

Dag turned in to it. It was one way and, luckily, it was his way. He drove passed the guy needed to find somewhere to park. Delivery lorries were taking up any available spaces that weren't used by street-side eating or seating areas. He turned into the semi-circular piazza and managed to find a parking space almost outside the pub he and Finn had used.

He looked in his mirror until he saw the guy walking into the piazza, waited a moment, and then got out of the car to follow him.

As he got out, Rolf phoned him. Dag quickly updated him and Rolf told him to follow but not to approach the man. He would be along in a car shortly to join him.

Dag kept his distance. The young man crossed the Piazza and headed straight for the City Hall. He crossed the square with the statue and fountain around which the Hall was built, and went directly up some steps, through the doors and into the building.

Dag stood by the fountain wondering whether to follow him in. He looked back towards the semi-circular road that ran around the piazza and, close to the incline leading to the Hall a car stopped. Rolf got out and it drove away to the side and parked. Rolf walked quickly up the incline and joined Dag.

"He's gone inside." Dag told him. "Shall we go in?"

"I don't want to alert him. That will be no good to us at this stage. We need to know what exactly he's up to. And he is the one – or so we think – who might be able to lead us to Finn and Anette. Don't forget that. So, best we make discrete enquiries with reception."

They went inside. Dag kept to one side and left it to Rolf to ask questions at reception.

"She knew who I meant. That's not surprising, he's quite distinguishable. He works here evidently; in the planning office."

Dag stared at Rolf for a moment. "He what?" Dag asked.

"He works here, in the planning department." Rolf repeated. "Why?"

"Finn's contact here worked in the planning department. The one he asked if there was anything important about to happen, or any special visitors. His name was Kenneth. I don't think he ever mentioned his surname."

"Let's go for a coffee." Rolf suggested. "I don't think Kenneth will be leaving the office until lunchtime at the earliest. I want you to go through everything Finn told you about this Kenneth. Meantime I'll ask Randi to find out all she can about him. Easy enough to get his work records for a start."

Dag;s usual pub wasn't yet open and there were no cafes directly on the piazza. They had to go to a cafe on a corner at the opposite side of the City Hall where there was what looked like a main entrance but remained unused and faced out onto another open space overlooking Oslo Fjord. A few people were sat at the stools and dry bars that looked out onto the fjord so Dag and Rolf choice a quiet spot at an ordinary table and chair on a raised platform at the rear of the cafe.

"So," Said Rolf when they had settled, "tell me all you can remember about Kenneth and Finn, try and leave nothing out, as you know the smallest of details can be important."

Dag tried to remember when Finn had first mentioned Kenneth.

"It was when Finn and myself both first looked around the City Hall; at the security cameras that were marked on the map. I wondered then if there were any important visitors or events happening. We looked on the internet but found nothing. That was when Finn mentioned Kenneth. He said they had gone to school together, so they must be the same age. And Kenneth had got a job working at the City Hall in the planning department. The next day, I think it was, Finn said he'd called Kenneth and had persuaded him to find out. It had been difficult, Finn said. Kenneth was wary about giving out any confidential information. It was the next day when Kenneth phoned Finn. That was when we were meeting, remember?"

"Yes." Rolf nodded.

"It was a couple of days later that Finn said he was going to meet Kenneth for a drink. We'd given up doing anything else useful that day anyway. They'd gone out drinking and to a club. Finn got back to the hotel in the early hours, three a.m. I got a text from him to say he was back safely. He didn't get up until late the next morning. It was when we went out that day that we were stopped by the Embassy car and Safia spoke to us about the map. Afterwards, when we were going over things, I asked Finn if Kenneth had come up with anything new, and Finn said that he hadn't. I don't think either of us has mentioned Kenneth since."

Rolf finished his coffee. "It's possible that Kenneth tipped off the Embassy. But why? He said there was nothing to tell you, but was there? Was he keeping something from you and Finn? Or did he tell Finn, but Finn didn't tell you? Were Kenneth and Finn in it together or was Finn an innocent party? And there's also the question of Anette; does she have any connection with Kenneth. Does Kenneth have any connection with the Church?" We've got ourselves an awful lot of questions, Dag."

There's only one thing I'll say. "Dag told him. "And that is there was nothing in Finn's demeanour to suggest that he was in anyway involved, or knew about, anything to do with the map.

I'm sure of it. I can judge a persons character, and it just isn't him."

Rolf nodded. "He could have been coerced after he made initial contact with Kenneth. Was there any change in his behaviour?"

Dag shook his head. "Nothing that I can think of, no."

Rolf's phone pinged. "Right," he said, "I've got a man in position, he can keep Kenneth under observation."

His phone pinged again and Rolf spent a while reading it. "Some info on Kenneth. Larsen's his surname. Same age as Finn, and yes, he went to the same school. His father also works for the Council, probably how he got his job. That's interesting; he attends a course to do with town planning at the University. That's a link for you. He'll be there tomorrow. That may give us a chance to see what he gets up to there."

"I don't really want to wait until then. Finn and Anette have been missing for a day now." Dag said.

"Yes, but only a day. You know yourself that the police would not normally be too involved at this stage. And we've had no contact, which is actually a good thing. If there was a reason to use them as some sort of lever or as hostages in some way, I think we'd have been contacted by now. No, I think playing it softly, a waiting game is best just for now."

"Finn's bound to think I'll be doing all I can to find him. He knows I wouldn't be just sitting on my hands doing nothing." Dag insisted.

"True. Then, if you were a policeman on this case and knew nothing I'd told you, what would you do? Besides talking directly to Kenneth, that is."

Dag sat back and thought. "There's not much in the way of leads is there? I'd go back to Anders' place at the very least in case there was anything I'd missed; try and find out where he was."

"Very well, you do that, and we'll keep Kenneth under observation. And if you do actually find out anything new, let me know."

Dag drove to Slependen. He parked outside Anders' house, tang the doorbell in case there was a reply, but there wasn't, then looked through the downstairs windows. There was no sign of life.

"He's not in. He's gone out" Came a voice from behind him. It was the neighbour Klara Sahlberg.

Dag turned. "Oh, it's you. I was just wondering if he was back." The thought. "You say he's gone out. So, he must have returned then."

"Oh yes, came back last night, I was just going to bed and closing my curtains, that's how I happened to see him."

'I bet.' Thought Dag.

"Went out again just as I opened them again this morning. Not that he was in his own car though. Someone dropped him off

227

last night and picked him up this morning."

"The same car?" Dag asked.

"Looked like it. Not that I'm any good with cars, mind you. It was a big one though, black. Like people drive off-road."

I see, thank you. I was hoping to see him. Finn and Anette haven't been around have they?"

"Not since I saw you last, no. There's nothing wrong is there? He's a strange man that Anders."

"No, I just couldn't get Finn on his phone. That's all. Must be broken."

Dag smiled thinking she might go away. He said nothing more.

"Oh, well." Klara said after a few seconds. "I've got things to do. I must be going."

"Yes, you go. I'll be fine." Dag smiled.

There was not much chance of him getting into the house with her spying on him. She'd be calling the police. But he had some information. Anders was moving around freely and being driven by someone. Well, maybe freely, it just depended on who was driving him. But whoever it was had left him at the house overnight, so they weren't worried about him being at liberty. And why did Anders spend the night at the house? Was there something he needed to find there?

He walked to his car, and as he was about to get in his

phone rang. It was Rolf.

"We've been watching for Lageson so we can have a word with him. But I think it would be a better idea if you did. We don't want to go in ourselves just yet and alert him. He's turned up at his Church; wondered if you'd like to go and have a chat with him? Ask him about Anette and Finn."

Dag agreed. He told Rolf he was finished at Anders' house and what the neighbour had said, and set off for the Church.

As this was a weekday there were many more cars parked along the streets outside the business units and the Church. Dag imagined that thee workers took advantage of the fact that there was unlikely to be any services and therefore worshippers, so took advantage of it. He had to park some distance away and as he walked towards the Church there was no sign of anyone being there. But, one of Rolf's people must have known the pastor was here.

He first tried the office door. That was the most likely. But it was firmly locked, so he went to the Church door. It was unlocked. He opened it as quietly as he could remembering that it had a creaking sound. He looked in around the partly open door. Lageson was there, at a solid table below a large cross that acted as an alter. He was knelt down. At first Dag thought he may be praying but then it looked like he was merely rummaging around the bottom of the table.

Dag pushed the door. It creaked. At the same time Dag coughed to announce his presence.

Lageson jumped to his feet knocking his head against the table and shouted, "Ow". Rubbing his head with a hand he stared at Dag and demanded, " What are you doing here? What do you want?"

"I wanted to talk to you." Dag replied.

Lageson's eyes narrowed. "What about? I've nothing to say to you."

"It's about my family." Dag said, taking a seat to show that he wasn't going anywhere very soon. "I've lost contact with them. I wondered if you had any idea where they may have gone?"

Lageson walked a few steps closer, and off the platform from where he preached. "Why should I know? And if I did, why should I tell you? You are a disbeliever who clings to the coattails of the authorities. You and your kind brings nothing but sorrow to the world and cover yourselves with the pretence of caring. Anders wants nothing to do with you, nor Anette."

"And Finn? What about Finn?"

"What about him?"

"Finn was happy to know me, be with me, but now he's gone missing."

"Missing? He went missing when he spurned the Church. That was when he became lost."

"So, do you mean he's not lost now? That he is no longer missing?"

"If he has found the truth through Christ's Testament he will not be lost."

"I warn you, if you know where Finn is, or Anette, you must tell me, or I will involve the Police." Dag threatened him.

"And will they torture me until I speak? Of course not. I will say nothing. Arresting me will make no difference."

'So,' thought Dag, 'he knows where they are, and he has every intention of not saying.'

"Is Anders with them?" Dag asked.

"None of this is any of your business. If, they were on a religious retreat it would be none of your concern. So that is what they are doing. Satisfied?"

"Satisfied? No, not at all. But for the moment you've told me what I needed to know, thank you." Dag smiled and stood. "But if you are holding anyone against the will, or under duress, I make you one promise, you will not get away with it."

Dag turned and walked out. He was absolutely sure that Lageson was behind the family's disappearance. And thinking back to what the neighbour said about Anders appearance the previous night, he was also sure that Lageson was the driver of the car.

As he walked back to his car, he looked at those parked about. There were several black four-wheel drive vehicles, and he quickly jotted down their numbers, although surely Rolf's people should now have it anyway. He couldn't see the Church from where he had parked his car, but sat in it to see if he saw Lageson take two of the three cars that were still in his view.

He waited. Neither of the two cars moved. He waited for

another twenty minutes, then got out and checked whether the other car was still parked. It wasn't. That was Lageson's car, he was sure of it. All he had to do was check the Church door to make sure. It was locked.

Dag went back to his car. It annoyed him that he hadn't seen the car drove away and been able to follow it, but sent a text to Rolf with the car's registration number.

"We have him under observation," Rolf said. "but he's just gone back to his house. If he sets off anywhere else, we'll be on to him."

"Didn't you have him under observation last night?" Dag asked.

Rolf cleared his throat. "There was a bit of a mix-up. An admin one. He was left unobserved for a while. During that time he made that car journey. We're checking traffic cameras now."

"Nice to know we're all not perfect." Dag said caustically.

They were sat in Dag's favourite cafe. The day had slipped by and it was mid afternoon. Within an hour or so the sun would be setting.

Rolf got a call. Dag waited to find out if it was a relevant one.

"They picked his car up ion some cameras. He headed towards Møllerveien, where Kenneth got on and off the bus." Rolf told him once the call ended.

"So, that's the area we must concentrate on. And we know that he'll be going to the University tomorrow."

19.

Dag had arranged to meet Rolf at the University the next morning. Rolf had made a point of telling him that, although the course usually took place further out towards the suburbs, it had temporarily been relocated to the Faculty of Law, the building not far from the Grand Hotel and Parliament building, only a short distance for Dag to walk. Evidently there had been a severe boiler breakdown, an explosion almost, knocking out all the heating and causing the dispersal of classes. Very suspicious.

"We've spotted him going in," Rolf told Dag, "a few minutes ago."

"Can we take a look around?" Dag asked. "For example, I'd like to see where the Peace Prize takes place in relation to where Kenneth's class is."

"Good idea, let's go in."

Rolf took him around the side of the building and an entrance there. Rolf's ID got them quickly past a check at one of the doors. Then, he took him to the hall where the ceremony would take place.

"It's large." Admired Dag. "How close is it to the road outside?" By the way they had come in and turned, he had gathered that the far would be next to the main road.

"Near enough, but easily closed off. There are fences around most of the area, and they can be just as easily patrolled. It's the main façade that's open with that piazza in front of it. But again the road in front of it can be relatively easily closed and barricaded. But it's not the view of things the Nobel committee would like to see. So much sign of security and force doesn't actually go with a Peace Prize, does it?"

"No. And the hall itself would be thoroughly checked beforehand, obviously."

"Of course."

"So, where is Kenneth?" Dag asked.

"The other side of the complex. Nowhere near here. But he'll be followed, and we'll find out if he's up to anything. The next thing is where he lives. We've found out where it is, I think we should go there. It took a little time, he's only recently moved, and he's move about a lot before as well. It's just around the corner from where he caught the bus."

"Finn and Anette may be there." Dag said, looking to see Rolf's reaction.

"Possibly. But for now we keep at a distance. If they're there, they'll be in good health, I'm sure. What we have to do above all else is get to the point where Kenneth gives away what he's up to. I've not got anyone spare to keep his apartment under observation whilst he's not there, though."

"Well, let's go and take a look."

They parked between in a space that was between a gap in the apartment blocks. The blocks surrounded a communal garden area. It was on the opposite of where Kenneth had caught the bus into town.

"They must be in his apartment. I can't think where else they'd be." Dag said when Rolf had pointed out where it was, although it was partly hidden between the surrounding blocks.

"You're not going in." Rolf reminded him. "Not yet at any rate. If we don't get any other info in the next twenty four hours then, fair enough, I think we might take the chance."

Dag was frustrated. He was confident he could have found out what was going on if only he was allowed to act. But he had no choice. Well, he did, he could have gone ahead anyway, without Rolf's approval, but he realised how that might risk the whole operation. He had to wait.

"So, what else can we do?" Dag asked.

"Wait. Sometimes just waiting, not doing, gets more results. Wait, and see what information comes in. We're still observing Lageson. He might also lead us somewhere. So, it's a waiting game. It's not as if the ceremony is going ahead any day soon. We've got time."

Dag spent the afternoon in his room staring from time to time at the white that he'd had brought up from the borrowed room.

Kenneth was still a bit of a linchpin, and they still did not know who 'Tocha' was, unless it was in fact Kenneth, but Dag doubted it. The Churches were also key. But were they directly involved or being used by this Tocha or the Brigadier perhaps? If the ceremony was going to be disrupted, how seriously? He suspected it was serious. A bomb was possible. But would that be the weapon a Church would use? If Lageson was anything to go by, Dag thought it was. Then, there was Anders. How was he being used? How deeply was he involved? And had Anette been coerced or indoctrinated into being part of it. Finn, Dag believed, must have bee persuaded to go with Kenneth because of his sister, and could only still be missing if it were against his will or if he was trying to protect her. That would mean Kenneth couldn't be holding them himself. If he'd left them alone in his apartment, Finn would have escaped and brought Anette with him if at all possible, Dag was sure of it. No, he was now convinced that Finn and Anette were not at Kenneth's apartment, they were somewhere else, and Finn, at least, being held against his will. The finger of suspicion pointed away to Lageson or the Brigadier and maybe his aide ,or perhaps Safia.

Rolf had mentioned that Lageson was still under observation, but what about the Brigadier, his aide, or Safia? The Brigadier was unlikely to be directly take part, so that left his aide or Safia. Dag picked up his car keys. He knew where Safia lived. He would keep an eye on her himself that evening and night.

Dag parked in much the same spot as he had before with Finn and settled down for the night. It was dark, cloudy and cold, and he'd managed to get some sandwiches and a Thermos from the hotel kitchens.

There was a trickle of people coming and going; mostly coming, as people returned home from work. Safia was one of them. Dag looked at the time. It was 19:00.

The time ticked by slowly. It was nearing 21:00 when Dag's eyes almost shut, and he jolted awake and poured himself some hot black coffee. As he did so, someone came to the apartment block door, rang a bell, then talked into the speaker. Their back was turned to Dag but there was something familiar about the person. As the lock opened the door, the person turned. It was a woman.

Dag stared, not quite believing who it was. The face was lit up by the inside light as she went in. There was no mistaking who was going in. But was she seeing Safia? Maybe, it was someone else who she was visiting? That would be a coincidence. In fact, Dag thought, too much of one. There was only one person she could be visiting; Safia.

Dag sat transfixed with the coffee cup going cold in his hand. Absent-mindedly he drank it without tasting it. His mind was trying to work out the probabilities, and there was not one which he liked very much.

All he could do for now was wait. Wait until she left. Then, he would have to follow her or decide if he should confront her. He resisted the decision to confront her; he would follow her, and go she where she led him.

It was half an hour later the door opened and she left.

She turned around the corner of the building onto the street and out of site. Dag waited a few moments and then started the car. He set off and turned the corner looking out for how far ahead she was. He couldn't see her. What he saw at the junction at the end of the road was a black 4 x 4. She must be in it. He accelerated to catch up. When he got to the same turning he saw the car at the end of the road to the left at the junction with the main road, and as he sped up to catch up with it it turned right into town.

What he had not been able to see clearly was the number plate. The air was warming and the windscreen was steaming up so that he had to put the aircon on full blast.

He got to the junction. The car was already well ahead to the right. Luckily there was no traffic and he pulled out without stopping. He sped up. The black car had just made it through a traffic light and Dag was stopped by it. There was no traffic and, tapping his fingers impatiently on the wheel he was tempted to pull out. But he waited.

The lights changed and his foot hit the accelerator. He raced along the road breaking the speed limit, taking a chance that he wouldn't be stopped. He caught a glimpse of the car. It had gone passed the gardens of the Royal Palace and were turning left at a roundabout. He followed, getting closer to it.

He and it went passed the rear of the University Building then turned right passed the Methodist Church that Safia had said she'd attended. They continued along the main road, Dag keeping a decent distance. They were heading back towards the Railway Station and Dag's hotel when the car turned left, and soon, left again.

Dag new the road. He guessed where the car was going. It was heading towards Kenneth's apartment.

As he approached the apartment block Dag slowed, keeping an eye out for the car. He drove around the block to where he and Rolf had parked before, and there was the car.

He found somewhere to park nearby and sat in the car, thinking.

It wouldn't be a good idea to go to the apartment and have a confrontation. It might be dangerous. It would be foolish. He had no idea what was behind what he had seen. He could come to a completely wrong conclusion, but he wasn't sure what correct conclusion he could come to. He was confused.

There was only one thing to do. Leave things as they were for tonight, and get Rolf to meet hi first thing in the morning. If he wasn't able to explain what was going on, or unwilling to, then he would have to take things into his own hands. He was beginning to think that he had lost all ability to see through things, to analyse complicated situations, as this one had become, that he had simply lost the talent that he'd had. It dented his confidence.

20.

Dag waited impatiently for Rolf. They had arranged to meet again at the cafe. Rolf had promised to be there by 09:15. Dag was there early and sat with his usual strong, black coffee, continually glancing at his watch seeing the seconds tick by.

Rolf was late. Dag was almost at the point of calling him when at 09:35 Rolf came through the door. Dag merely nodded to him. Rolf went to the counter and got himself a coffee, then came to the table.

"Sorry I's a bit late. You sounded, how shall I say, tense, when you phoned. I told you I'd let you know if there was any news." Rolf told him.

"It's me who has news for you." Dag said.

Rolf waited for more but Dag stayed quiet. Rolf frowned. "And what news is that?"

"I couldn't just hang around the hotel last night, so I decided to do some observation of my own." Dag began.

"Hmm, well, I told you it was bets to leave it it for now."

"Best for whom?"

Rolf's frown returned. "You've something to say, Dag. What is it."

"I decided to keep an eye on Safia; parked outside her apartment." Dag paused.

"OK, well, did anything happen? I imagine it did. This must be leading somewhere. Get on with it."

"I saw someone go in. They must have been going to see Safia. There was no-one else they could possibly be there to see." Dag told him.

"One of our suspects?"

"No exactly, no."

Rolf's frown returned. "Not exactly suspect, but someone we would both recognise by the sound of it? You're dragging this out Dag."

"The woman stayed for about half an hour then left in a black 4 x 4."

"A diplomatic car?" Rolf guessed.

"No. At first, I thought it was, but it had no CD plates. I followed it."

"Hang on, you haven't said who it was." Rolf complained. "Let me guess, was it Ingrid?"

"I followed the car," Dag continued, without answering the question. "It went to Kenneth's apartment."

"Anette?" Rolf guessed again. "Surely she's too young drive? Or if she isn't, she wouldn't be driving a car like that."

Again Dag did not reveal the answer. "I am sure she is directly involved with Safia and, probably, Lageson through Kenneth. Either that, or I have been sent on some sort of wild goose chase."

Rolf's eyes narrowed. "You haven't confirmed either of my guesses, and there's only one other woman I can think of. But that's something I'm loathe to believe."

"Yes, there's just one other woman; Randi. That's who I saw. There was no mistaking her. Who is she working for Rolf? You? If not, I don't like the implications; you would have been using me for some underhand reason. And I don't want to think that. On the other hand, if that's not the case, you've got a problem."

Rolf sat back in his chair and stared at Dag for a moment.

"I've got a problem." Rolf agreed with a sigh. "I'll talk to Torje, I'll need outside help, someone not part of our department. Don't do anything until I get back to you. Act as if you know nothing of this. I can't have any other compromises."

"Very well. But I don't want this hanging over us for days. Today, fair enough, but after that we, or I, will have tom take some action. It can't go on any longer."

Dag went back to the hotel. He sat in his room with the white board in front of him. He saw the code name, Tocha, and wondered if that could be Randi; Randi working on the inside, knowing all that they knew, given every chance to counteract anything they found out or to distract them from the truth. But what was the truth, the whole truth. Dag felt even more so now that he didn't know. Anything that he had thought might be the truth, might not be. And what of Finn and Anette, and of Anders, and even perhaps Lageson? How did they really fit into all of this? Finn must have been coerced into leaving Dag, probably using his sister as a pawn. But what was her part in it? She was only young, she surely could not be a key player. He father, more probably. And then there was Lageson. In Dag's mind it all swirled around him and his own Church's links to that of Africa, the Brigadier, and of course, Safia, who must be working in conjunction with with the Brigadier and with Randi. It was a mess.

He cast all these thoughts out of his mind. His only concern now must be the safety and welfare of Finn and Anette. But all he could do was wait for Rolf to contact him.

He had gone outside into the square and its gardens outside the hotel to get some air when Rolf phoned. He asked to meet at the usual cafe and said that Torje would also be with him. Dag looked at his watch and set off right away. It was only a few hundred meters away. He would be in plenty of time but it would enable him to get an extra coffee in before them came. He took a seat in the far right hand corner from where he could see out of the windows covering the crossroads outside.

It wasn't only Torje who turned up with Rolf, but Ingrid as well.

"I've had to let Torje take the lead." Rolf began. "I can't trust disclosing any plans to my own guys and I've had to allow them to carry on keeping the same people under observation as if nothing had changed. The other thing we decided, as you can see, is that we have brought Ingrid into this. You may be wondering why?"

"I'd have thought you'd keep this to yourselves." Dag said.

"We've decided to keep it very much 'in-house'. And we four are that house. We are going to be the team which brings all of this to a conclusion. A tightly-knit group who can operate, how shall I say, a little more independently than might otherwise be the case."

Dag raised his eyebrows. "Not like you. And are you sure," he added, looking at Ingrid, "that we are all working to the same end?"

"I can assure you Dag, that we are." Ingrid spoke for herself.

"We have agreed a plan." Rolf said. "But this is a bit public." He added as a few more customers came in. "Torje has arranged somewhere we can use."

Torje took them to an anonymous office block on a corner of a side street not far from the Parliament. The windows were of the one way mirror type that, from outside, reflected the sky and surrounding buildings. There was no sign on the door, just a keypad entry system which Torje used keeping his back to the others.

Torje stopped the group at a reception desk, and they were given passes to wear around their necks. Torje's had a picture of himself on it, the others simply had the word 'visitor' written on them. They took a lift to the third floor and then Torje took them to an office. It was bare except for a table and chairs, a large TV screen, several phones of different colours sat on the table together with a computer tablet and keyboard.

"So," Dag said, having been quiet during their walk to the office, "what's the plan?"

"Rolf took the lead. "As I said, we can't let Randi know that we know about her, I've had to keep most of my guys out of the loop, although my superiors are aware of the problem. But what we have done is set up tracking on Randi. Interestingly she sometimes turns her issued phone off, although it's not unusual if there's a security risk to it being on. However, we have found out that she regularly uses another mobile, so we are tracking both of them. At the moment she is off shift for two days, so whatever she's doing it's not connected to work. Torje?"

"I have set up a small team strictly under the need to know principal. What we would like to do, is track her, and the other players, until they meet. But if she goes to Kenneth's address again that will also trigger a response. Hopefully we can catch her and Kenneth together and discover if Anette and Finn are there. Even if she meets Safia or Captain Fadika there's little we can do about them because of the diplomatic immunity, so we're hoping that she goes to Kenneth's. Personally I would have liked to find out more about what they're up to before moving in on them, but we'll have to move and depend on interrogations to get that information. Now," He said standing up and turning on the big TV screen, "let's see where she is."

The screen lit up showing a map of Oslo. At its centre was their office highlighted by a blue dot. An orange dot blinked at Kenneth's address. Several other small yellow dots were arranged around the map. One near Kenneth's. One close to the street where Safia's Consulate was, and another close to a pulsating red dot. That was Randi. It was stationery.

"She's at home." Rolf explained.

She lived in an apartment about three kilometers North West of the office beyond the Palace Park, just inside the ring road.

"So, now it's a matter of waiting." Said Ingrid.

"I'll order some coffee and sandwiches." Torje told them picking up the phone.

The afternoon dragged on with no movement from anyone.

It was at 15:30 that things began to happen. Safia's tail began to follow her on foot as she left the Consulate. At the same time Randi's tail called in to say that she was on the move.

Safia was walking towards the parliament, not far the office where they were sat. Dag wondered if they could look out of the window and see her if she passed by. She could easily have been going to meet with the Brigadier at the Grand Hotel. But she wasn't. She had taken a left and a right and halted at a bus stop. The tail had her in his sights but held back. A number 54 bus came. Torje typed in the bus number and its route cam up on the screen overlaid on the map.

"That's a bus to Kenneth's." Dag said, uttering the obvious.

Meanwhile Randi was driving her car. She had gone the short distance North and onto the ring road heading clockwise.

"If she carries on around it she can turn off and head down to Kenneth's." Said Rolf, interpreting her move.

"We shall follow her." Torje assure him. "But we must be careful, she has training in spotting and shaking off trackers."

A line of text appeared at the bottom of the screen. 'No movement.' Beside the words blinked an orange dot. It was a report from the agent at Kenneth's.

"They're both going there." Dag said. "I can feel it."

"I'll have a car waiting outside." Torje told them. "Just in case. The bus will take about twelve minutes, and if the ring-road is clear," He looked at his watch. "About twelve minutes for Randi if that's where she's heading."

"I think we should just accept that is where they are going and make a move." Rolf said.

Torje agreed and they bundled out of the office, down the stairs, instead of waiting for the lift, and out into the street where a black 4x4 was waiting. Torje had grabbed the tablet on his way out and sat it on his lap. It showed the same screen as in the office, but this time there was a new dot – their car.

"It'll take us eight or nine minutes, so we should be there about the same time or just after." Torje informed them. "It would be quicker if it wasn't for all these one-way streets."

Torje was in the front seat next to the driver. Dag and Rolf tried to look over his shoulder to see the tablet screen.

A thought came into Dag's head. "What about Lageson?" He asked. "Have you got him under observation?"

"My guys are doing that, as well as the Brigadier and Captain Fadika. I had to give them something to do." Rolf told him.

"And do you know what they're up to?" Dag asked.

"If they are on the move I'll be informed, don't worry about that."

The dots on the screen had moved. Randi was still on the ring road and coming towards the turn off for the road to Kenneth's. The bus was only half-way there. Their own car would catch up with the bus by the time the bus got there, and they might arrive at the same time as Randi. All of them, arriving together.

"We'll have to hang back and let them go into Kenneth's." Torje said. "No good arriving too early."

"There's a place you can park with a good view." Dag pointed towards the screen. "There, a slip road just across the road, with parking spaces at the top."

"OK." Torje agreed. "My observer's in an apartment facing

Kenneth's but I don't want us to be seen entering it. He can relay any movements to us."

Torje had brought up a 3D satellite image showing The dots converging on Kenneth's apartment. It zoomed in slowly as the dots moved closer together, converging on the apartment.

They overtook the bus as it stopped to let passengers on and off, and they sped ahead. Randi had come off the ring-road and was heading down the main road towards town and their destination. It now looked as if they should be there before she was.

Randi and their indicators closed. But they were now ahead of her. The bus was further away.

They passed the apartment blocks and turned right at a roundabout, then right up the slip road incline turning into a parking area. As the engine died they could see Randi arriving at the roundabout. They looked out of the windows and from between the leafless trees that formed a barrier between them and the main road, they saw her go around the roundabout and find a parking space alongside the apartments. She got out, looked around, checking out the area, then walked between two blocks to the entrance to Kenneth's.

Torje's hand-held radio which had been in the car, crackled, and the observer reporter Randi going into Kenneth's block.

They now had to wait for the bus to drop Safia off, but that would be at the other side of the apartment blocks. They would have to wait until the observer reported seeing her.

It was then that Rolf's phone rang. He listened,

"Lageson's on the move." He reported.

"He could be coming here as well." Ingrid suggested.

"That means we'll have to wait." Torje told them. "We can't go in and alert them until we know if he's coming here, and if he is, get them all at the same time."

"What if they break up before he comes?" Ingrid asked.

"Then we go in anyway." Said Rolf. "If it looks like it, we'll have to be quick on our feet."

"Wouldn't it be best to take up positions now?" Asked Dag. "I could go then other side of the apartments and station myself there. It's only Safia who is likely to go that way, but I don't have any authority to hold her."

"Hold her. She may complain, but let her. We can let her go afterwards if she claims her immunity. Ingrid can go with you." Rolf told him. "Torje and I can be ready by Randi's car, just over the road, in that driveway. It might be where Lageson will park as well."

"Here." Said Torje, taking an extra handset from out of the front glove box, and passing it to Dag. "Keep in touch."

"OK. Let's go." Agreed Dag. He and Ingrid could wait at the bus stop where he had looked out for Kenneth before, acting as if they were waiting for a bus.

As they left the car, Rolf's was on his phone again. "It seems like Lageson's heading this way. I'm ordering my guy to park by our car. He doesn't know Randi is here."

They were in position. No-one had emerged from the apartment, and Lageson was now not far away.

Dag saw a car coming from the direction of town. He recognised it. Hastily he spun, turning his back to it, and grabbed Ingrid in an embrace.

"Lageson!" He said as the only explanation he could muster.

For a second she struggled and then relaxed.

She laughed. "I haven't heard that one before. Where is he now?"

"Going round the roundabout. He'll be looking for a parking space."

Dag had already pressed the button on the handset and told Torje.

"He's parking. I think we may as well move in as soon as he's inside." Torje replied.

They waited.

"He's in." Torje said over the handset. "We'll move from our side, you from yours. We'll see each other as soon as we enter the courtyard garden."

Each pair came to the courtyard. Torje told Dag that the entrance to Kenneth's apartment was a door in the middle of the central block overlooking it from the opposite side. His observer, stationed in the block on their side, reported that no-one was looking out of Kenneth's window. They were free to cross the courtyard to the door. They briskly followed a path alongside the side blocks and to the door.

"He's on the third floor, at the top, that balcony to the right." Torje pointed.

The door was, as usual, controlled.

Torje pressed one of the buttons. A woman answered. He said he was from the post office and the package was too big to leave in the letter box, and asked to come in. Without checking, she let him in.

"Why are people so easy to fool?" Dag shook his head.

But already Torje was leading them up the stairs; one flight, two, then three. The came to Kenneth's door. Torje and Rolf listened. They could hear muffled voices from inside.

"I think a direct approach." Said Rolf, taking a pistol from under his coat, as did Torje.

Rolf rang the bell.

The voices quietened. Rolf rang it again, for longer this time.

Dag stood to one side behind Rolf, Ingrid the other behind Torje.

They heard a key on the lock and a slow turn of a door handle. The door opened by a crack.

"Who is it?" A voice asked, presumably Kenneth.

Rolf gave no reply, and gave the person no chance. He barged the door. It burst open, Rolf with it, his hands holding up his weapon pointing at whoever was behind the door.

The person behind it was, indeed, Kenneth. The door had slammed against his face, and he had fallen backwards and lay prone on the floor, blood coming from his nose.

Rolf took no notice of him, but bounded over him and headed towards what must have been the lounge. Behind him was Torje, then Dag. Ingrid was last. Dag turned to Ingrid and pointed to Kenneth and telling her to watch him. Dag wanted to follow behind Torje and be there when they found Finn and Anette.

Within about five steps and less than half a second Rolf was standing at the edge of a door with his weapon pointing into the lounge. Torje had taken up a position on the other side of the door, weapon raised ready to move. Dag came up behind Rolf also ready with his pistol.

Another heartbeat and Rolf stepped into the room. Torje stepped to one side to come in behind him with his weapon now pointing into the room, and Dag pressed up behind him to look inside.

"Weapon down!" Shouted Rolf.

Dag peered in. Randi stood at the other side of the room with her own weapon raised, pointing towards them. For a fleeting moment her expression was one of surprise and amazement, turning into one of bewilderment and confusion.

"Put it down!" Rolf repeated.

Randi was now facing three weapons. She was not stupid. She had been trained. There was no point doing anything else other than to obey. Her arms fell, and when the pistol was pointing to the ground she dropped it.

Now Dag, from being transfixed by Randi, looked around the room. In the opposite corner, behind a sofa, were Lageson and Safia. Dag turned his weapon onto them and followed Rolf who had taken steps into the room.

Rolf went to Randi, turned her around, and was taking out handcuffs. They could see into the kitchen and it appeared empty. Torje was heading into a bedroom to check it out. Dag moved up to face Lageson and Safia.

"Where are they?" Dag demanded.

Both of them had looked in shock, now a puzzled expression crossed their faces.

Dag repeated the question.

"What do you mean?" Lageson asked. "Who?"

"Finn and Anette. Where are they?"

"Finn? Anette? I don't know what you mean." Lageson said with a dazed shake of the head.

"Where are Finn and Anette? It is a simple enough question. Just answer it." Dag demanded.

"I've told you. I don't know what you mean. I have no idea what you are on about. Why should I know where they are? You are the one who has seduced them away from their father. Why don't *you* know where they are."

It was Dag's turn to frown. His body relaxed and he lowered his weapon as Torje came back into the room.

"All clear." He announced. "No-one else here."

Torje took over. "You two, you're under arrest." He told Safia and Lageson.

"You can't arrest me, I have diplomatic immunity." Safia insisted.

""We can arrest you and hold you until your Embassy or Consulate confirms your identity." Torje told her.

"Then what is the charge?" She demanded.

"If you have diplomatic status it's activities incompatible with that status, until then it's conspiracy." Torje told her.

Safia fell silent. Lageson had not said a word.

"You've nothing else to say?" Dag asked Lageson.

"Nothing." Lageson replied and stood defiantly and tight lipped.

Torje was on his handset. His team who had been following Randi and Safia were heading up the stairs. Rolf had stood down the man who'd followed Lageson; he didn't yet want any of his people directly involved.

They bundled them together and led them out of the

apartment.

Torje's men had arrived. Rolf looked about for Ingrid and Kenneth expecting them to be waiting for the others.

"Where's Ingrid and Kenneth?" Rolf asked.

The arrivals looked at him blankly. "Who?" One of them asked.

"There were two other people here. A man and a woman. Where are they? Did you see them?" Rolf said urgently.

One answered. "I saw two people walking that way." He pointed towards the gap between two apartment blocks leading to the bus stop. "A man and a woman."

"Shit!" Rolf swore, and Torje also cursed.

"Get after them!" Torje ordered the man who'd spoken. "Now!"

21.

Dag sat with a member of Torje's team at a desk confronting Lageson. He had repeated the questions regarding Finn and Anette, but Lageson was sticking to his story that he knew nothing of their whereabouts. Dag had to leave any further questioning of him to Torje's man.

Dag puzzled over it. He wasn't just puzzled he was mystified. If he didn't know where Finn and Anette were, where were they? The only connection there had been was that Kenneth had seemingly picked up Finn outside the church. Kenneth was the connection but he had been spirited away by Ingrid. Rolf had been a fool to trust her; so had he, and so had Torje. What had she been up to? What was her connection to Kenneth; what use did she have for him? Obviously she had known a lot more than she had let on. Which made him remember the car accident – or rather the attempt on his and Finn's lives. Was that what it was, or was it just a set-up. The more he thought, the more questions sprang into his mind.

The only person who hadn't appeared in their sights that day was his brother-in-law, Anders. Where was he? Who had been keeping an eye on him? He was the only person left who could know of Finn's and Anette's whereabouts, other than Kenneth, who they could not question.

Dag had to wait to see Rolf. It was a half hour before he could ask him if he had a man watching Anders; he did not. Dag told him that he was going to Anders' house in an attempt to find him, and asked if he could put a call out for Anders' car. He had a feeling Anders would not be at home, but that if he found where he was he would also find Finn and Anette.

Dag pulled up at Anders house. Once more he rang the bell, once then twice, and looked through the windows. No-one was at home.

He didn't have to wait long before he had some answers at least. Klara Sahlberg, the neighbour, appeared again.

"Have you seen them recently?" Dag asked. "I've not heard a word from them."

"He came back once more after you came last time. I watched him."

"Did he drive or was he dropped off again?"

"He was dropped off again. The same black car, or one just like it. Didn't stay long, only about twenty minutes. Came out with two large suitcases."

"And you not heard or seen anything since?"

"Nothing, no."

"Well, thank you. Maybe they have gone on holiday somewhere."

"Never a one for holiday's, Mr Thomsen. All a bit strange if you ask me. Have you thought of calling the police?" Klara asked.

"Yes, I'm working with them. If you see or hear anything else, give me a call." He handed her one of his old cards with his mobile,on and the old Kristiansund Police office number blacked out.

Dag sat in his car wondering what to do next. It sounded very much like they could have done a bunk; gone abroad even. He needed Rolf to have a check done on flights from the airport, and sent a text to ask him. Rolf replied almost immediately saying that they were already doing so for Ingrid and Kenneth and would add Anders and his children to it.

For now, he was stuck with no leads. Unless the airport check found anything or Anders car was spotted, which was unlikely as he'd been driven by the mystery car, he couldn't think what else to do.

He drove back into town and parked the car. He could have waited in the hotel, but he needed a drink. He went for a walk.

Without thinking his feet led him to the City Hall and its piazza. So much had circulated around this place, but nothing seemed to be attached directly to it, nothing except those marks upon the map.

The pub on the corner of the piazza was open, and he went in for a drink.

He sat with a beer in front of him taking only one sip, and letting the rest settle so that the froth slowly diminished. He looked out through the window onto the piazza watching the people passing by. He remembered sitting there with Finn. He remembered sitting with him when he'd first spotted Ingrid go past. He remembered when he'd seen Safia and Captain Fadika go past and followed them. And it was where he followed Kenneth and the place where Kenneth worked.

Dag's phone pinged. He thought it might be news about Finn, but it was just Rolf telling him that Safia had been released after demands from her Consulate. She wouldn't be staying here though, they would be told that she was persona non grata and had twenty-four hours to leave.

Dag looked at his beer. It was getting flat. He gulped down almost half of it but couldn't stomach any more. He decided he needed some fresh air. As he stood to put his coat on his phone rang. He looked at the number but didn't recognise it.

"Hello." Dag said and listened.

"Uncle Dag. Is that you?"

It was Finn's voice.

"Finn! What's going on? Where are you?"

"Shh. Keep it down. I've got to talk quietly. I'm fine. I'm using father's phone. Your number was on it. It must have been when you phoned up about mum."

"Where are you? Where's your sister?"

"I've got to go." Finn said, and the call ended.

Dag couldn't risk calling it, Finn must have broken the connection because his father was nearby. But what he could do, now that he had the number, was get Rolf to do a trace.

It was an hour later that Rolf called back. He had the phone's geo-location. It was an address that Dag thought he recognised. He looked it up on his phone. It wasn't quite the same address, but it was very near, just a few doors away. It was just around the corner from Kristine's doctor, Sven Halvorsen. There was even a lane passed a couple of other houses leading to the doctor's surgery.

Dag sent a text to Rolf. He told him that he was going there. Rolf sent one back almost immediately asking him to wait. It would be better if someone could go with him, he shouldn't go alone. He would make a call and get help from the Oslo Police. Dag told him to try Detective Inspector Bjørn Solberg; he had already been involved in the map.

Dag waited another twenty minutes before Rolf, this time, called him.

"Bjorn will meet you outside the hotel in a few minutes. I've emphasised that it is tied to a matter of National Security and he would be acting on our behalf as well. He'll give you every assistance. But remember, if they are in any way linked to my investigation they will be turned over to myself and Torje. You understand that?"

"I understand."

No sooner had Dag opened the hotel door and stepped outside than a car stopped. Bjørn waved at him from the passenger seat. Dag got into the rear. In moments they were on their way to the address.

"I've another car coming." Bjørn told Dag. "Best be on the safe side."

Bjørn got the driver to stop the car on the pavement next to the house which was built on some slightly higher ground with a fence along the roadside that hid them from view. A little further away was a lane that led to the house entrance and wound passed a few more houses to the main road on the other side and the Docto's Surgery. The second car had parked there and two officers would come along the lane from that direction. Any escape from the house would be blocked.

They turned up the path to the house. Bjørn stationed the driver the first point, a parking bay and rear door. He and Dag went to the garden gate which led to the front door. Already the other two officers were heading towards them along the lane. Bjørn ordered on to join the driver. The other remained nearby.

Bjørn and Dag opened the gate and walked to the door. Bjørn rang the door bell. They waited. There was silence and Bjørn rang it again. This time Dag was sure he heard movement from inside. Dag nodded to Bjørn.

"Open up! This is the police!" Bjørn shouted.

There was a noise from the side of the building. Dag heard a shout form one of the officers there.

"Hands up! Stay where you are!"

Bjørn nodded to Dag, and Dag jogged along the side of the building to the parking bay and rear entrance. The officer on standby joined Bjørn at the front door. Anders was standing there, arms held out at his side, the two policemen confronting him with raised weapons.

Dag waved at the officers to put down their guns.

"Anders." Dag said. "Where are Finn and Anette?"

Anders looked pale, drawn and older than he had only days before, and gave a deep sigh as he spoke. "They are in there."

Dag nodded to the two officers who came forward to take him in custody. Bjørn came around from the front door.

"We'll go in this way. I've left the others at the front door. Nobody's come to answer it."

"Where exactly are they?" Dag turned and asked Anders.

Anders gave him a weary look, and for a moment Dag wondered if he was going to tell him.

"There is a cellar. They are there." Anders told him.

Dag turned, nodded to Bjørn, and they went in, Bjørn in the lead.

They didn't have far to walk. In the corridor just off the

kitchen where they had entered they could both see the door to what must have been the cellar. Dag opened it with the key hanging on the wall and called down.

"Finn – Anette – are you there? It's Dag. You're safe now. I'm coming down."

There was a muffled sound from below. Dag looked at Bjørn. Bjørn nodded and Dag took the lead going down the steps. Behind him Bjørn had found a light switch and harsh electric light broke the darkness.

First he saw Anette who was tied up and loosely gagged. Then, he heard a groan from a darkened corner. It was Finn. Bjørn went to Anette and Dag to Finn.

Dag took Finn's gag off at the same time as he heard crying coming from Anette, and Bjørn reassuring her.

"No talking." Dag said. "Let's get you out of here first."

Dag purposely left any questions until they got to the Police Station. He told Finn and Anette to calm themselves and wait until then. First of all they must be have a medical check to make sure they were well enough to answer questions. Anders was taken in a separate car.

Rolf joined them at the Station. Finn was first to be questioned. When Rolf was satisfied they moved on to Anette and then to Anders to get his side of the story.

The house belonged to the doctor, Sven Halvorsen. Anders had told him a story about a water leak and the boiler having to be replaced, and asked to stay in what he knew as the doctor's second house which he normally rented out. It seemed the doctor had, at some time, had a loose connection with the Church and did him the favour.

Anders had no idea about what his two children had become involved in. Finn, by chance, through Dag, and Anette through their pastor, Jorgen Lageson. Lageson had persuaded, and used her, as a messenger; Anette thinking is was Church business linked to his friends at a church in Africa.

It was Kenneth who was the surprise. Finn had not mentioned that Kenneth had also had a connection with Lageson's Church. Lageson was his uncle. Kenneth had, a few years ago, attended the Church, but had lapsed, or apparently lapsed. Clearly he hadn't.

Anders discovered that Anette had been running errands for Lageson, sometimes late at night, which had angered him. Then he found out that Anette had been meeting Kenneth. He thought there was something sexual going on and had lost his temper completely. Before Anders took Anette away from home for her safety, as he thought of it, she had managed to get a message to Kenneth. Kenneth had followed them and found out where Anders had taken her. It was then Kenneth went to find Finn and tell him what Anders was doing.

It was also when Finn found out that Anette was definitely being used. But, of course, he had known of her involvement before then, he just had refused to believe it. For it was Anette he saw g oing into Safia's apartment that night when he and Dag had kept it under surveillance.

"You should have told me. That was stupid." Dag told Finn.

Finn could only nod his head and agree.

Finn argued with Kenneth and accused him of being involved with his sister and with Safia. They were in the doctor's house. They had not thought Anders was there, but he was, and he overheard them. There was a struggle. Kenneth managed to escape but Finn hit his head and blacked out. The next thing he knew, he and Anette were tied up in the cellar.

Anette still had her phone on her. Her father had not realised. At that time Finn was tied up next to her. He managed to get his hands on the phone and make the call which Dag received. But his father came in, found the phone, and separated them.

"Well," said Dag, "your father will be charged with false imprisonment;the unlawful restraint of a person against their will. It's quite serious. We'll have to wait to see if he gets bail. It'll be OK for you, you're can look after yourself, but social services will probably want to put Anette with foster carers. I don't expect them to let her live with your father at the moment."

"She can stay with me." Finn said. "I'll look after her."

"And where will you live? You can hardly go home if your father is on bail, and they won't let him see either of you."

Finn looked at Dag and gave a slight smile. "You're a trustworthy person aren't you, Uncle?"

"I live in Kristiansund. That's too far away."

"Stay here for a while." Suggested Finn. "Unless you've got something important to go back to. But I don't think you have."

Dag sighed and shook his head. "I don't think so. I mean, it would be ..., well, it's not what I'm used to ...., I'm a loner really." He paused and his eyes met Finn's. Finn was not going to let him get away with any excuses, he realised that. "Well, I'll have to stay for a short while. I want to find out what their plans were; if Rolf will tell me that is."

"I've been thinking about that." Finn said. "It was something that Kenneth said to me when we were out having a drink. Thinking about it now, I'm sure he was trying to find out what we knew about the map. But he let something slip. He said that if there was an emergency then the Peace Prize would be moved to the City Hall. I think there must have been a plan to disrupt it at the University, then the map would make sense. They would already have planned for an attack there and not the university and no-one may have thought of that. The security would probably be lax. They could even have planted a bomb in advance of the change!"

Dag nodded. He liked the way Finn thought things through. "I'll give Rolf a call and tell him your idea."

Rolf listened.

"He's quite bright really, isn't he. Mind you he dropped a clanger not telling us when he saw his sister." Rolf said. "So, I may as well tell you his is correct. Lageson knew the plans and was partly behind them. He told us everything. He was almost gushing, keen to prove to us that he was in the right and everyone else, us that is, were in the wrong; only he could see the truth of everything as God had revealed it to him. A lost cause I'm afraid."

"But what about the others?" Dag asked. "Especially Ingrid and Kenneth."

"As well as Safia, the Brigadier and his Aide have been declared persona non grata. A word of warning has been whispered into President Rakha's ear. And Manasé Rabenarivo, the President of Nagamba, has also had a warning. It was made to sound as if we did not think he was involved, of course. But, surprisingly, the troops on both sides of the border have puled back. As far as Ingrid is concerned, we are still a bit confused. We were sure she was working for the major mining company, she had documents supporting that. But, knowing Ingrid, she could have been working for more than one side at a time and playing them off against each other. I imagine Kenneth knew more than she wanted us to know if we interrogated him so thought it was better to deal with him herself."

"Deal with him?" Asked Dag, concerned.

"We are still trying to trace him. There's no evidence yet that he left the country. I just hope that our worst fears are not substantiated."

"You think she may have disposed of him?"

"It's certainly possible. And we shall everything we can to get to the bottom of it. Not that we've found any trace of Ingrid either. But that's no so unusual is it?" Rolf mused.

"What about 'Tocha'?" Dag asked him.

"Do you know, I think that was Ingrid herself." Rolf pause,d then said. "What do you intend to do next?"

"I really should take some time to look after Finn and Anette. I don't think Anette should go back to her father, not yet ant any rate."

"They will be needed here as witnesses." Rolf reminded him.

"Yes I know. I suppose I'll have to stay here for a while, Find somewhere to rent. I can think what to do about my house in Kristiansund later."

"So you may stay here?"

Dag was silent for a moment. "No, I don't think so. I think I want to get away; away from here and away from Kristiansund. Maybe far away. One day, anyway. But sooner rather than later."

Characters

Dag Meldel – Ex Police Inspector

Martin Sorensen – Detective Inspector, Kristiansund Police

Jamba Caleb Rakha – President of Ikebaje

Kristine Paula Thomsen – Dag's sister

Anders Thomsen – Dag's brother-in-law

Finn Thomsen – Dag's nephew

Anette Thomsen – Dag's niece

Sven Halvorsen – Kristine's Doctor

Bjørn Solberg – Detective Inspector, Oslo Police

Rolf - E-tjenesten Agent – E14

Ingrid – Agent and previous receptionist at the Flåm Hotel

Kenneth Larsen – City Council planning office worker

Randi - E-tjenesten Agent – E14

Malidi Shomari Jata – Brigadier, Ikebaje Defence Attaché,
                     brother-in-law of the President.

Safia Mesay – Agent of Nagamba

Jorgen Lageson – Leader of The Church of Christ's
                Testament.

Manasé Rabenarivo – President of Nagamba

Klara Sahlberg – Anders' neighbour

Cpt. Fadika – Aide to Brigadier Jata

Torje – Government Agent

Tocha – The Torch, code name

Also by the author:

Dag Meldel Detective Tales:
The Arcturus Code – Book 1
Hagal's Eight – Book 2
Kickback – Book 3
Lost Overboard – Book 4

The Lazuli Fantasy Series:
The Lazuli Stone – Part One
The Lazuli Brotherhood – Part Two
The Lazuli Crown – Part Three
The Lazuli Inheritance – Part Four
Lazuli ~ The Fall of Albia – Part Five

Young Adult Science Fiction:
The Riddle Of Red Rocks – Part One
The Quantum Agency – Part Two

Silas Daniel Dyer – Biographical History

Stories of Lost Souls – Short Story Omnibus

Sterngard's Words – Science Fantasy